Midnight

Midnight

STEVEN W. WISE

Thomas Nelson Publishers
Nashville

Published in Nashville, Tennessee, by Thomas Nelson, Inc., and distributed
in Canada by Lawson Falle, Ltd., Cambridge, Ontario.

Scripture quotations are from the KING JAMES VERSION of the Bible.

Library of Congress Cataloging-in-Publication Data

Wise, Steven W.
    Midnight / Steven W. Wise.
        p.   cm.
    ISBN 0-8407-3454-9 (pbk.)
    I. Title.
PS3573.I798M5   1993
813'.54—dc20   92-2458
                                            CIP

Printed in the United States of America
1 2 3 4 5 6 7 - 97 96 95 94 93 92

For Lillie,
who loved many children.

Prologue

THE WOMAN felt no pain as the first greedy cells multiplied and claimed space that did not belong to them. Though the frenzied growth took place in a microscopic arena of flesh and blood, the promise of greater power was certain to its creator. Yes, they would do his bidding, these tiny warriors of evil, as they clustered like grapes on the vine. They would march slowly enough to give him great pleasure as her sighs of discomfort grew to screams of agony, and yet swiftly enough to satisfy his craving for her soul without undue delay. For in the end that was all that mattered to him—her soul, disentangled from the disgusting clutches of the Enemy. Her torment would indeed be entertaining for a time, but the day of death, that juiciest of morsels, would be enjoyed beyond measure. It was always so.

He watched as the night breeze tenderly moved the hair across her brow, and he cackled with satisfaction as the woman slept in ignorance. As he hovered over her, he thought with delight of others like her, frail beings inflicted with all manner of pain. He laughed at what she would become. This one was a prize of great value. She had long tampered with his plans for children, and he chastised himself for not coming to her sooner. But the time of retribution was at hand. He lingered a moment longer, cursing all of humanity, and then the Prince of Darkness swept from the room as silently as he had come.

Five hours later, the darkness of the room gave way to the colorless light of a North Carolina morning. Slowly, the small calendar hanging above the nightstand was illuminated. It was cluttered with scribbled notes, some written in ink and others in pencil. Dates were circled in hurried fashion, with some having small stars scrawled around them. It was a calendar which told much about the vibrant life of Lillie Crow during the month of November.

She awoke refreshed and full of love to give to the five children who still slept in the big house on Morningside Road.

And the invaders deep within her were relentless as they increased their mass and claimed more and more of her body during the dark months of winter.

1

WILLIS McCANT swung his legs out of bed and carefully tested the cold wood floor with bare feet. Despite the laborings of the oil-fired furnace, the April chill that had gathered over the Missouri River had crept into the house which sat five hundred yards from its bank. The man passed a calloused hand over his cheek and the raspy sound of flesh against a day's growth of beard filled his ears. He arose slowly and groped about the room for his work clothing and felt the familiar pangs as the muscles of his arms and shoulders protested the morning.

He glanced out the window before leaving the room. The promise of strong sunshine bolstered his resolve; his body would loosen easily at the job site and by mid-morning he would feel younger than his forty-seven years.

Three grade school children slurped cold cereal at the small kitchen table as he entered the room.

"Morning, you pups," he said.

Two of the three raised their heads long enough to smile at him, then quickly returned their attention to their bowls.

"There's a sweet roll that isn't stale yet. You want it with your cereal?" his wife asked.

"Why, yes, Emma, that sounds just great," he answered with mock delight.

The oldest child giggled at his answer, and Emma laughed easily with him.

"Guess I didn't make that sound too good, huh?" She paused as she put the plastic container of milk in the refrigerator. "Y'all still working at that old church building?"

"Yeah, but it ain't a building anymore," he mumbled through a mouthful of cereal. "We got to start cleaning up the foundation today. Then we can fill the hole and start on the new work."

"See that they get on the bus, will you? I'm going to be late for work if I'm not careful."

He nodded as she grabbed her purse from the counter and bolted for the back door.

Fifteen minutes later Willis squinted at the demolition site through the windshield of the old pickup. The brakes squealed in protest as he rolled to a stop next to the dirty yellow bulk of the backhoe. The operator, a squat red-faced man, climbed into the tiny cab and the engine roared to life, piercing the tranquility of the morning.

Willis worked near the bucket attached to the long arm of the backhoe, directing its placement with hand signals to the operator who could work at a much quicker pace with the aid of the extra set of eyes. Willis's boots made wet, sucking noises as he struggled for footholds in the muck. The great steel claw reached out like the paw of a gigantic beast and sought rotten timbers and jagged chunks of concrete. Willis reached down to wrestle a large section of concrete into the bucket when his eyes fell on a tiny chest, the size of a small breadbox. The operator swung the loaded bucket toward the bed of the waiting dump truck. Willis took three muddy steps to the object and stooped over it for a closer inspection. The lock was firmly in place and, though battered and caked with filth, it appeared sound. In the few seconds before the backhoe pivoted back to face him, he made the decision to say nothing to the backhoe man. They would be working away from the spot now. The chance that it contained anything of value was slight, he reasoned, but he could not help feeling a tingle of anticipation. It was a chest, and it was locked; there must be something in it. He had found it, and he would decide what to do with it later. There was no wrong in that, he assured himself.

The remainder of the day passed uneventfully. He was unusually quiet at the supper table, prompting a raised eyebrow and a comment from Emma, but he dodged it with an oblique reply. After the table had been cleared and the children planted in front of the television, he spoke of his strange find.

STEVEN W. WISE   [11]

"Emma, I saw a little chest stuck in the mud at the church ruins this morning."

"A chest? What kind of a chest, Willis?"

"Oh, probably it ain't nothing. Just a little thing, but it still had the lock on it. I . . . I didn't say nothing to Charlie on the hoe. Just left it there."

They passed ten seconds in silence before Willis made his intentions known.

"I'm going to go back and get it. What do you think? I'm the one that found it. That old holy roller church has been knocked down for twenty-five years or more. Can't nobody be around that owns it."

"Maybe you ought to turn it in to the company. . . . I don't know . . ."

"Turn it in so fat cat Earl Denning can check it out? No, no . . . I'm not about to do that, Emma. A man finds something that old, I figure it's his. Oh, there won't be nothing in it worth a dime! What am I getting so worked up about anyhow?"

"You going to go get it?"

He paused and nodded silently before he reached for the denim jacket hanging on the back of the door.

The flashlight beam probed the darkness as Willis picked his way through the sticky earth. The big man squatted beside the chest and with his left hand rocked it free of the clinging soil. He carried it to the bed of his pickup and wiped away the bulk of the mud with an old towel he had retrieved from

MIDNIGHT

under the seat. Then he latched the tailgate of the truck and quickly drove home.

After the children were tucked in bed, Willis brought the chest into the kitchen and placed it on a section of newspaper. He had broken the small lock off with a hammer before bringing it indoors. With Emma watching from the opposite side of the kitchen table, he raised the lid and they both peered inside.

"Now if that ain't something to get worked up over," he drawled. "I'll declare."

He shook his head and laughed scornfully as he looked across the table at his wife. She made no reply as she studied the two objects resting side by side. The old Bible was badly worn. Most of the leather cover had rotted away. The faded purple of the thin page marker protruded from the bottom of the pages. Emma reached in and withdrew what appeared to be a four-inch square blank picture frame. The glass cover was cracked from one corner to the other, but the wood frame, though crudely made, felt sturdy in her hand. She rotated the frame slowly to see if some image could be discovered in the dirty white background.

"Looks like a piece of cloth under the glass," she said.

"It must have backed a picture, I guess," Willis offered.

"No, I don't think so," the woman said thoughtfully. "Look at the back. It's sealed perfect. Why would anybody take out a picture and then go to

STEVEN W. WISE [13]

this much trouble to seal the frame back up? They meant to frame the cloth. Had to have. It must have meant something to somebody, but who in the world knows what?"

She extended it toward Willis and as his huge hands touched the wood and glass he felt a deep remorse, strangely penetrating, nearly haunting. Clearly shaken, he clumsily replaced the frame inside the chest and took a deep breath.

"What's wrong?" Emma asked.

"I . . . I ain't sure." He stole a glance inside the chest before continuing. "I just know I had no right messing with it. It means something to somebody from that old holy roller church."

"It might, but I doubt it. They're probably all dead by now. There hasn't been any holy rollers around here for a long, long time."

"That's so, I know. But there might be an old one left around here somewhere, and I'm going to find out."

Emma looked at him inquiringly, and he could not evade her silent question.

"I just don't know exactly why. Stop looking at me like that, will you. I know I ain't no church-going man, but that don't mean I can't do something decent, does it?"

"For pity sake no, Willis. I didn't mean no harm. Calm down. I think it's a good thing, too. I'll help you look for somebody."

Emma reached across the table and soothingly patted the massive knot of clenched hands. She reached into the chest and withdrew the tattered Bible. With great care she opened the cover and squinted at the faint lettering at the top. The ink was badly faded but legible.

"Willis, there's a name in it. Look."

She turned the Bible around for his inspection.

"Cora Whitten, ah, something, it looks like," he said.

"Whittenburg is what it says, I'm pretty sure, Willis. Cora Whittenburg was the woman who owned this book."

"Even if she's dead, she might still have some kin around somewhere. It's a good start, ain't it, Emma?"

The woman smiled at him and nodded in silence.

Two miles away, the only sound at the old church site was the whisper of the cool night wind as it swirled about. Aloft, it pushed before it the great clouds that hid the moonlight. But the waxen light sought the place, and for a moment its splendor found the earth, illuminating the sodden ground. Then the eye of God withdrew into the heavens, and night reclaimed the place.

♦

Five months had passed since the mutant cells deep within Lillie Crow's right breast were given life—given life so that her life might be taken. The tiny dot had doubled in size twenty-one times.

This would be a day of both sadness and joy, she mused as the pancake batter began to smooth in the big plastic bowl. Division of Family Services had called two days before with instructions to have the child ready by ten Monday morning. A permanent foster home had been found for Tina Livingston. Lillie had become attached to the six-year-old with the face of a tiny angel and the little mouth that could smile now. The child had been at Crow House for over a month, but the smile had appeared only within the last few days.

"Surely to hope her next years will be better than her first six," Lillie whispered aloud in the big kitchen.

On the morning of the child's arrival from the hospital, her feet were hidden beneath the white bulk of bandages. Everything was under control now, the county health nurse had assured Lillie. Tina's feet would heal nicely. The nurse had come daily to change the dressings, and after two weeks soft socks and cloth slippers sufficed. But it had taken two more weeks before the magical love of Lillie Crow had brought the first smile.

Long ago Lillie had learned to ignore her own first touch of hatred toward abusive parents, but those of this child had tested her resolve. Liquid bleach, the nurse had told her. They had held the child's feet in a bowl of bleach as punishment for the blisters that had resulted from running in too-small shoes. Neighbors, who finally had heard one too many screams from inside the house trailer, had called the police.

The batter was ready for the electric skillet, and

as the first pancake oozed into shape, the tall woman whispered again to herself.

"Thank goodness the screams of a child are a hard thing to ignore."

The two-year-old was taking a nap when the car pulled into the driveway. The other three young-sters were frolicking over the small playground in the fenced backyard. The social worker was a petite, high-spirited young woman named Susan Kelly. She had formed a bond with Lillie during the past two years of her service in the Division, and the two had worked out an informal routine for small children that nearly always made the difficult moment easier. The big front door swung open.

"Good morning, Susan," Lillie said.

"Good morn . . . why, Lillie Crow! You didn't tell me that Tina was the prettiest girl in the whole wide world!"

The child's hand was lost in Lillie's, and she looked nearly straight up into the eyes of her pro-tector as the smile began to form at the corners of her mouth.

"Isn't it so, Susan. And her heart is as pretty as her face, I'll tell you."

Lillie squeezed the child's hand gently as she knelt beside her.

"Tina, before this day's done, there's going to be three happy people together. You know that, don't you, baby doll?"

The girl nodded and glanced at Susan's face and back to Lillie's.

STEVEN W. WISE   [17]

"Tina, two of the nicest folks I've ever met are waiting to see you, and they are full of love," Susan said.

"Ha! There, she said the word!" Lillie yelped in delight. "What's our rule, honey?" She extended her hand in front of her and began to chant the word in slow cadence as she counted with her fingers.

"Love . . . love . . . love . . . love . . . love . . . love."

Lillie lowered her voice to a whisper so that Tina's squeaky utterances could be clearly heard.

"Why did you say that pretty word six times?" Susan asked in mock surprise.

"Tell her, child," Lillie urged gently.

" 'Cause . . . 'cause I'm six years old," came the faint reply.

"That's going to be our rule from now on, Susan. First time we hear somebody say 'love' every day, we're going to repeat it however many times we've had birthdays. Isn't that right, baby doll?"

Tina nodded and looked at Susan for approval.

"Why, that's the best idea I've ever heard, Tina. I'll bet you helped Lillie think that up, didn't you?"

"I'd never have thought of it in a million years by myself," Lillie interjected.

"There's only one thing wrong with it that I can think of, Tina," Susan's eyes danced at the child. "It will take Lillie half of her morning to count to sixty. . . ."

"Why, you young pup. I don't feel a day over thirty-five!"

Tina was giggling at the exchange between the two women and covered her mouth with tiny cupped fingers to hide the laughter which was sweet music in the big room.

"Tina, you'd better take this young lady away from here before she gets me riled up, okay?"

The child nodded as Lillie wrapped her in strong arms and whispered in her ear. The woman's nostrils were filled with the fragrance of lilac shampoo and her heart was touched by the trust she sensed in Tina's embrace. She swallowed against the lump in her throat.

"It gets better and better from now on, little one. I promise. You can believe Lillie."

Within seconds, the dainty woman-to-be was at the car door, and then she was gone. Lillie allowed the warm breeze to dry her eyes as she watched the car disappear around the curve of the road, and she fixed yet another small face in her memory. And with the face, a tiny pair of bandaged feet.

She turned quickly and walked with purposeful strides toward the backyard where the three children played in the Carolina spring morning. There would always be more coming to live in Crow House. Of this, she could be certain.

Lillie had been the children's surrogate parent for the twelve years that Crow House had been in existence. It was founded to fill a gap in the system that local law enforcement officials had long lamented. When children were taken from abusive parents, or the parents were placed in custody by authorities,

STEVEN W. WISE   [19]

the children were taken to the police station or the county sheriff's office for immediate care. Although the officers were compassionate and gentle, they were still uniformed giants to the children, with guns and night sticks hanging from their belts, and the austere station house could be of little comfort to traumatized children. A loose network of volunteers had offered their homes as temporary havens, but it had proven difficult to match the steady stream of youngsters with the few who were willing to tolerate the disruption of their families.

Led by the police and sheriff's departments, the town had finally united in the worthy effort of finding a better solution. Funds were raised to acquire an old two-story house at the north edge of town. Volunteer labor set about the task of renovating the house inside and out as the newly formed board of directors began the search for house parents. Their search led to Lillie, who was working in the local nursing home. One of the board members who regularly visited his mother in the home had observed Lillie's firm but loving ways with the elderly, many of whom, in the lonely autumn of their lives, were like troubled children. It had proven to be a perfect match. Lillie had welcomed the change in her life, and with the sight of the first child entrusted to her, the woman who had been denied children of her own felt a bond form. She knew she had found her place for life.

The breeze teased the tight curls of silver on her head as she watched the happy activity in the backyard. Nearly six feet tall in the prime of her life, Lillie was still an imposing figure, even though the years had taken nearly two inches from her slightly bowed frame. Her bone structure was more typical of a man's, and long muscles had formed through years of hard work. Though lacking any real beauty, the features of her expansive face were pleasant. The wide-set hazel eyes were striking, always dancing in animation with her spirit. Her frowns, which were infrequent and never without purpose, were marked by two deep lines extending upward from the bridge of her strong nose.

She looked down at the long fingers wrapped around the top brace of the chain link fence and shook her head in resignation. With the slightest flexion, the great knuckles protruded, craggy and white. They were hands she had been ashamed of in her youth, and she had sought to hide them at every opportunity. But then the beautiful summer came, so long ago now, and with it came the great hands of George Crow. He had wrapped his around hers and made them the hands of a woman again. She smiled at the memory of him that summer; a sweet, gangling giant of a man who made her laugh and love, and who had married her in the fall of nineteen forty-nine. He had trusted in a God of eternity and goodness, but had never attempted to overpower Lillie with his own beliefs. Whatever power had given him to her had quickly taken him back half a world away in North Korea. His flesh turned to memory on a frozen mountain pass just south of the Chosin Reservoir on the sixth day of December, nineteen fifty.

She had never recovered that part of her, the part that sang with the unbounded joy of womanhood, nor did she desire to recover it. When the Korean mountain consumed George Crow, it took the part of Lillie that was her husband's alone. In the first months after his death, dark thoughts tormented her spirit and drained life from her. But there were other mourners in the winter of nineteen fifty, and they clung together and cried together and sought the spring together. When the trees budded out and the wind lost its sting, Lillie knew that only in the giving of herself could she be set free. She must lose her life in the lives of others. In so doing, she would find her own.

The laughter of the three children arose from the yard, and Lillie knew that they could laugh only because they had taken a part of her, a part willingly given, and she joined in their laughter.

MIDNIGHT

2

IT HAD taken Willis over two weeks to locate someone who could direct him to a former member of the old Pentecostal congregation. There were few hours during his week that were not taken by work or family, but he spent them diligently. There were no Whittenburgs in the phone directory, and he made his search through calls to pastors of other churches. They provided names of elderly members who might have knowledge of the old church. After sixteen days of fruitless labor, as the supper dishes were being cleared away, Emma asked the question that led to Hattie Wells.

"Willis, have you checked over at the nursing home?"

"No," he replied, shaking his head thoughtfully. "No, and I can't believe I haven't. Why didn't you think of that sooner, woman?"

The next evening Willis gulped his last bite of supper and dashed out the back door, heading for the nursing home. The receptionist glanced up at him pleasantly as he stopped in front of her desk.

"Good evening, sir. Can I help you?"

"I hope so. Do you have anybody here who might know something about the old holy roll . . . er, uh, that old church up on Lankford Road? The one that's just been torn down."

The woman paused and thought for several moments before speaking. "Well, there is one resident who might, but . . . Let me get the nurse. I'll be back in a moment."

She returned with the night duty nurse who walked directly to Willis.

"I understand you want to talk with Hattie Wells?" she asked.

"Well, I didn't exactly know who she was, but . . . the lady there . . ."

"Yes, the receptionist told me why you want to see her, Mr.?"

"Willis, ma'am, Willis McCant," he answered.

"Hattie isn't doing very well, and when she isn't entirely with us, she has ranted some about her Pentecostal background. I'm not sure it would do any good to try to talk to her. She's ninety-seven years old, and her mind comes and goes. Is it really important that you speak with her?"

"Yes, ma'am, it is. It really is," Willis said, and he did not try to hide the urgency in his voice.

The nurse pursed her lips and exhaled lightly as she looked at the big man wringing the cap in his hands.

"Well, I suppose you can try. But if she becomes agitated, I'll have to ask you to leave. Do you understand?"

"Yes, ma'am. I promise. I won't get her worked up."

The nurse led him over the polished vinyl of the long hallway to the last door on the left and preceded him into the semi-lit room.

"How're you doing, Miss Hattie?" she asked softly.

The old woman did not reply as she slowly turned her head toward the voice.

"You have company tonight," the nurse continued. She motioned toward Willis who took a tentative step forward and swallowed deliberately. He looked into the cloudy eyes straining to focus on his face. Thin lips moved up and down over toothless gums as the eyes continued to stare at Willis. He glanced at the nurse, but without further word, she moved toward the door.

"I'll be just down the hall," she said and left the room.

Willis turned back to the woman and drew a jagged breath before speaking. "How do, Miss Wells. My name's Willis McCant. I . . . I hope I won't be no bother to you, but . . . I . . ."

A long, blue-veined hand, more bone than flesh, crept from the tangled sheet and beckoned him. He took the step to her bedside. Only a few wispy strands of white hair clung to her scalp, and deep crisscrossed wrinkles were etched in her pallid skin.

STEVEN W. WISE   [25]

Willis looked into her eyes again, and noticed they had cleared discernibly. The voice was raspy with age, but clear when she spoke.

"What took you so long, young fella?" she asked.

"I beg your . . . pardon . . . ma'am."

"It's all right, young fella, I knowed you'd come. Danged if you didn't about wait too long though," she said as the beginning of a tired smile formed at the corners of her mouth.

Willis felt the first chill creep up his spine, and the woman sensed his discomfort.

"It's all right, I tell you. I'm not crazy. They think I am, but I ain't. I get loud when I talk to the Spirit sometimes, but ain't nothing wrong with that. No, ain't nothing wrong with me but age." She paused and rested for a moment before continuing. "Cora's been on my mind for long days, now. Yes, she has."

Willis gasped and felt the rising thuds within his chest as the woman looked directly into his eyes.

"Poor young fella," she said soothingly, "you ain't never been close to the Spirit, have you? Sit yourself down in that chair. You look plumb peaked in the face."

Willis gathered himself and drew the chair under him before she continued. "Strongest woman I ever knew, Cora was. Holy Spirit lived in her. I can tell you that. You ain't going to find her though. Been gone long years now. But I'll tell you where to find Carl; that's her son. He's still alive, I know."

She paused for breath again, and Willis could hear faint wheezing sounds come from her chest.

"Lives two streets east of the old church, Carl does. About even with it. Won't be much of a house by now. You'll find it."

Willis could not speak, but he managed a nod. Several minutes passed and the only sound in the room was the rough whisper of her breathing. She turned her head toward Willis for the last time and found his eyes.

"Listen," came the hoarse whisper, "the singing's getting louder. I want to be alone now, young fellow. You look where I told you. You'll find him."

He stood on shaky legs and fumbled with the chair. He wanted very much to say something to her, but did not trust himself to fight the growing lump in his throat. He managed to reach the door before the weary voice stopped him.

"Take the Bible and the cloth both. Take them both."

He staggered, half running, down the corridor and burst through the lobby and out into the cool evening. He drew in the refreshing air in long, hungry breaths before making his way to the pickup. Ten minutes passed before he trusted himself to drive home.

Emma looked up inquiringly as he entered through the back door.

"Any luck?" she asked.

He nodded without speaking and sat down heavily at the kitchen table.

"I found her son, Cora Whittenburg's son, Emma.

There's an old woman in the nursing home . . . This is gonna sound wild, but . . ."

He stopped and pressed both hands to his face, massaging his temples with his fingers.

"Sit down, Emma. I got to tell you what happened over there."

◆

The nurse had watched Willis's hurried departure with surprise, and quickly walked to the room at the end of the hallway. Though her breathing was labored, the woman appeared to sleep peacefully.

Fifteen minutes passed before the nurse returned to check on her. But when she stepped through the doorway, she knew it was over. The room was silent now—deathly silent. She walked to the bed, and after checking for a pulse, gently pulled the sheet over the woman's head. She closed the door behind her and walked to the nurse's station. The receptionist watched and listened as the nurse spoke briefly on the telephone in short sentences and then hung up.

"Poor old thing," the receptionist said.

"Yes, she was. I don't know what kept her alive for the last two weeks. It's hard to predict with some of them."

"What did that man say his name was?" the woman asked. "I didn't pay attention," the nurse replied. "I can't remember names anyway. We ought to try to call him, I suppose, but . . . Durant. I think it was Durant. Look in the phone book."

The nurse watched as the woman ran her finger down the page.

"No Durant here, Linda," she said as she looked up.

"I don't suppose it matters anyway. He wasn't a relative. Just let it go. Poor old thing didn't have anybody."

The nurse paused and shook her head.

"It's a shame when they die without their minds like that, you know?"

The older woman nodded a silent reply and walked back to her desk.

◆

After a short search the next evening, Willis located three houses appearing to be likely possibilities for the house of Carl Whittenburg. As he drove down the street a second time, the slow-moving figure of an old man emerged from one of the houses. Willis slowed the pickup and then stopped as the tires rolled unevenly over broken pavement at the edge of the street. By the time Willis had walked to the three steps leading to the small front porch, the old man had seated himself in a metal lawn chair. Three days' growth of white beard enwrapped cheek and jaw. He was bald except for two untamed knots of hair extending like pointed wings from either side of his head. The years had carved deep

diagonal lines across his cheeks that were accentu-
ated by tired flesh. His eyes were not foreboding,
but they peered intently from under the bushy eyebrows at the stranger before him who held a small
chest.

"Evening," Willis said, throwing up a hand in
greeting.

"Evenin' to you," the old man replied as he returned the gesture.

"Are you, by chance, Carl Whittenburg?"

"Not sure it's by chance, son, but that's who I
am," he answered in a steady, bass voice.

"Well, sir, my name's Willis McCant, and I think
I found something that belongs to your family."

"No family left but me, Mr. McCant."

"Yes sir, I . . . I mean it was your ma's, this Bible I found."

The prominent bushy eyebrows moved downward as the man squinted intently at Willis, and the
dark eyes were persistent and unblinking. He rose
slowly and extended his hand to Willis who offered
his own and shook hands.

"Sit down won't you, son?" he said, motioning
toward the empty chair beside him.

Willis eased his bulk into the chair, carefully securing the chest in his lap. He opened the top and
withdrew the tattered Bible, then placed it in Carl's
open hand. The long fingers enveloped it lovingly.
Willis watched the old man's face intently as he
mouthed hushed words. His head bobbed slowly as

he squeezed his eyes shut for a moment before looking again at his visitor.

"I reckon the old cloth is in there, too?" he asked, his voice choked with emotion.

Willis nodded and handed the small frame to Carl. He inspected it carefully, running his fingertips down the crack in the glass cover.

"That crack was there when I found it, Mr. Whittenburg. I . . ."

"It's all right, son. I know you took good care of it." Carl paused and looked up into the bud-covered branches of the silver maple that soon would shade the yard.

"Where'd you find these things?"

"At a job site. We were clearing away the foundation of that old holy . . . er, church."

"Holy roller church?" the old man interjected, and laughed easily. "It's all right, son, you can call it that. It won't hurt my feelings. It was holy and we did roll some, that's for sure. But that was a long time ago. Folks got real smart as the years went by. No need to get loud and scare the neighbors, they said. So everybody got smarter and the church got quieter, and the neighbors quit complaining."

He paused and looked into the tree branches. "And the Spirit left the place, and He left most of the people. Old holy rollers. Lord, Lord, yes, we were that in the strong days."

He looked at Willis and smiled, and his eyes danced with the memories.

"Momma and Miss Hattie Wells, they were the

strong ones. Don't reckon you've run across Miss Hattie in the last few days?"

Willis could sense the same uneasy feeling begin to crawl over him that he had experienced the night before in Hattie's room.

"Well . . . yes. Yes, sir, I . . . she was the one that told me where you lived. I was . . . well, me and my wife, we was just looking for an old person who might have heard of your momma."

"I figured that was who it was," Carl said. "I got to get over and see her again before long. She's mighty feeble these days, but there's nothing wrong with her mind."

"Yes, sir, that's true enough. Her mind was good last night."

Suddenly Carl sprang from the chair, the Bible in one hand and the frame of cloth in the other.

"Lord God!" he shouted, "those two were something in the old days. Praying and healing and singing to the rooftop. They were the only ones who knew where the old cloth came from, and they wouldn't tell. Not Daddy, not the preacher. Nobody. 'Ancient', they would say, 'Ancient is the cloth. That's all anybody needs to know.'"

He threw back his head and laughed at the memory. Then, closing his eyes, he drew the cool air deep into his lungs and exhaled loudly. He glanced down to Willis in apology.

"Don't worry, Mr. McCant. I won't get cranked up. Somebody around here would likely call the police."

Willis stood to leave as Carl reached to shake his hand.

"I'm sorry I got carried away, son. I didn't mean to scare you. You've done a fine thing, troubling yourself to find me and bring these things here. I'm beholdin' to you. I surely am."

"I'm glad I did, Mr. Whittenburg. Wasn't that much bother. I just felt the need to do it. I ain't sure why."

"Oh, I know why, son. I know why."

Willis looked into the shining eyes for the last time and quickly walked away. As he neared his pickup, the old man's voice sang out across the yard.

"You come back sometime when the sun's high and hot, you hear? I squeeze a fine pitcher of lemonade. We'll talk some more."

Willis smiled back at him, but did not reply. The roar of the engine shattered the peace of the evening, and once again the old man was alone on the porch. He turned and entered the house, walking directly to the tiny bedroom with the oak dresser nestled in the corner. The oval-framed photograph was black and white, its subject formally attired in a high-collared blouse, buttoned to the top. Her dark hair was drawn up atop her head in a tight bun. Her features were strong, yet womanly, and the deep-set eyes bore out of the past with a force that belied the lifeless paper image.

"The old cloth came back, Momma. There's a woman standing in the need somewhere, and the Spirit and me, we're going to find her."

He sat down on the edge of the bed and opened the tattered Bible at the page marker to the fifth chapter of Saint Mark. He ran his finger down the page to the twenty-fifth verse and began to read aloud.

> And a certain woman, which had an issue of blood twelve years, and had suffered many things of many physicians, and had spent all that she had, and was nothing bettered, but rather grew worse, when she had heard of Jesus, came in the press behind, and touched his garment. For she said, If I may touch but his clothes, I shall be whole.

Carl placed the open Bible on the bed and knelt before it. As night overtook the room, the only sounds were the whispers of an old man's prayer.

◆

For the third time in the last half hour, Willis glanced at the lighted square face of the small alarm clock on the nightstand. The hands read ten minutes before midnight, but sleep would not come to him. He listened to the peaceful sound of his wife's rhythmic breathing, but it did not matter. He wrapped his right hand around the point of her shoulder and shook her awake as gently as he could manage.

"Emma . . . Emma, I'm sorry, but I got to talk."

She rolled onto her back with a long sigh. "For pity sake, Willis," she said wearily, "I've got a hundred things to do tomorrow, and you want to talk? It's the middle of the night. What time is it?"

"You hadn't been asleep that long. I'm sorry . . . but . . ."

"Willis, I'm telling you, it's just not worth getting worked up over. Let it be. You did a nice thing for an old man. But now it's over. So just let it rest."

"I'm trying, Emma, but I just can't get those two off my mind, especially that old woman in the nursing home. It was spooky, the things she knew."

"It was just coincidence, I'm telling you, her thinking about an old friend and her Bible and things. You think God swooped down and told her?"

"Well, you didn't see her or hear her like I did. It was plumb strange around her and the old man both."

"How else do you think you'd feel around religious fanatics, Willis? These people've been hooting and hollering at the sky like a bunch of coyotes all their lives. Anybody would have felt strange. Now please hush up and get some sleep."

She rolled onto her left side and, after two irritated tugs at the cover, silence returned to the room.

"I reckon you're right," he sighed in resignation, "the feeling will surely go away. You're probably right."

Without turning over, Emma reached behind her

STEVEN W. WISE   [35]

and patted his stomach. "Trust me, Willis, it will. Now go to sleep."

And in the night, long before dawn claimed the room, the seed of the Spirit withered and died, never again to seek root in Willis McCant's soul.

3

SUMMER CAME early and the coast of North Carolina began to swelter. By the end of June the humidity hovering at the edge of the Atlantic combined with unseasonably high temperatures to irritate even long-time residents of Washington. The central air conditioning unit that had been installed in Crow House four summers before hummed efficiently as the mid-morning sun devoured the shadows. Lillie watched contentedly through the kitchen window as the twin boys romped in a circle around the swing set. The baby, a two-year-old girl, sat in the corner of the kitchen amid a colorful collection of plastic bowls and wooden spoons.

"Pretty good stuff, huh, baby girl," Lillie cooed at the child who smiled with delight as she banged a spoon on the vinyl-covered floor.

She had cared for the six-year-old twins for two weeks and the baby for nearly three with practiced ease. But the phone call an hour before had put her in a thoughtful mood, one that would allow her to marshal the resources she would soon need with the arrival of a girl named Kay. She was ten days from her thirteenth birthday, a child who had been the secret, captive mistress of her father for a length of time known only to the girl and the man.

She came with the first shadows of evening. Two dull thuds of car doors being closed summoned Lillie to the front window. She watched Susan walk quickly around the car, place an arm around the girl, and begin to guide her gently toward the front porch. Lillie squinted in the fading light and studied the round face framed with dark, straight hair. The features were plain, without expression, and the girl's eyes seemed to be fixed at a point a yard in front of her shuffling feet. She wore a sleeveless dress of poor quality, which Lillie judged to be a size too large, but it did not conceal the delicate roundness of womanhood that had come disastrously early.

Lillie opened the door and stepped forward to greet her new dependent.

"This must be Miss Kay," she said softly as she reached down and took the girl's right hand in her own.

"Yes it is, Lillie," Susan said. "Kay, this is Miss Lillie Crow, the lady who will take care of you for awhile until we can get things sorted out a little better for you. I'm sorry we're running a little late, but . . ."

"Great day Susan, it doesn't matter one bit, except

that you two missed the best fried chicken dinner in North Carolina."

The women glanced discreetly at Kay for any reaction to the lighthearted comment, but there was none.

"Let's get you settled in, child," Lillie said as she wrapped an arm around Kay's shoulders, careful to withhold the full weight of it.

"I'd better run," Susan said. "You'll be fine here, Kay. I promise, honey."

The girl made no reply and continued to stare at the spot in front of her. Susan gave her a final, reassuring pat on the shoulder, and smiled grimly at Lillie as she turned to leave.

"Are you hungry? We've got one of those fancy microwave gadgets that'll make that chicken sizzle again in just a minute."

The girl shifted her gaze slightly and finally shook her head almost imperceptibly.

"Well, anytime you want, it'll be waiting. Come with me and let's get you settled in. I've got the big corner bedroom all ready for you, with the prettiest light green bedspread you've ever laid eyes on. And wallpaper, why, you've never seen anything like it!"

Lillie slowed her pace as they began to climb the stairs, and Kay soon fell into step with the tall woman who continued to chatter soothingly. By the time they reached the top stair, the girl lifted her face and stole a furtive peek at Lillie, who pretended she didn't notice. Once in the bedroom, Lillie handed Kay a packet with a new comb, a brush, a cellophane-wrapped toothbrush, and a small bottle of perfume. Nail-bitten fingers caressed the items, and one by one, she placed them carefully on the dresser. They had rested there for only a few seconds when she took the perfume bottle in her hand. The tears came suddenly, but there were no sobs with them and, except for the quivering of her chin, the small face was like stone.

Lillie resisted the temptation to find the reason for the tears, and in the silence, Kay handed the bottle to her. "Lord knows you're tired out, child. And me blabbing at you like my tongue's come loose. You lie down and get some rest. I'm going to tend to the other children for a while. My bedroom's right next to yours, and the bathroom's next to it. I don't go to bed very early. If you need anything, just let me know."

After some games and a bedtime story, the twins and the baby were tucked in for the night. As Lillie prepared for bed, her thoughts were with the girl in the corner bedroom. She anguished over the fact that she had been unable to break through the defenses of the wounded child. She tucked two pillows behind her and read a book for an hour, absorbing very little of the narrative. As the clock in the living room chimed eleven, she noticed the small figure silhouetted in the dim light beyond the doorway. Without a word, Lillie placed the book on the nightstand, and extended both arms to the child. The girl bounded over the carpet and threw herself onto the bed, weeping bitterly. The two rocked as one and Lillie made no attempt to stifle the great sobs. Five minutes passed before they began to give way to sniffles; Lillie reached for a box of tissues. Two more minutes passed in silence before the girl spoke her first words in Crow House.

"He . . . he always made me put on . . . perfume . . . before . . ."

"Hush, child. It's all right now. It's all right. You're with me now."

With the passing of each day, more of the girl's wounds were soothed by the gentle woman who was no stranger to grief. Lillie made certain that Kay had enough responsibility to prevent brooding, and yet not enough to cause any pressure. She quickly became attached to the baby girl and, under Lillie's tutelage, soon became proficient with feeding and bathing. The mysteries behind flaky pie crusts and light, tender fried chicken were unraveled in the bright kitchen, and in the sultry dusks the porch swing creaked in harmony with the tree frogs and crickets as the child bonded with the woman. On her seventh night at Crow House, Kay announced with a hint of pride in her voice that she would sleep alone. By the tenth night, Lillie noticed that all the lights were turned off in Kay's bedroom, and Lillie thanked the spirit of goodness that a child's capacity for anguish, however great, was limited.

Morning came without portent of crisis. Kay awoke to the sounds of the twins roughhousing in the kitchen as Lillie prepared breakfast. The aroma of waffles teased her nostrils as she listened to Lillie's voice regain control of the kitchen.

"My last warning, you two pups. It's been a while since I sat on anybody, but I'm just before doing it again."

The commotion soon died away with the threat and by the time Kay entered the kitchen, the scene was peaceful.

"Kay, cut up the baby's waffle for her, will you, hon? She's poking it down like a little pig. Easy on the syrup. As soon as we get these three filled up, we'll sit down to a little peace and quiet, okay?"

Kay nodded her approval as she finished cutting up the small square of waffle for the impatient baby girl who was whining at the delay. Within minutes, the boys banged out the back door. Kay put the baby down in the corner of the kitchen and took the plastic bowls from behind a cabinet door, making a colorful ring around the child. A muffled hiss filled the room as the hot lid of the waffle iron seared the thick batter. Lillie had turned to reach for the coffee pot when she stopped and cocked her head toward the low-pitched rumbling of a car engine on Morningside Road. The car slowed discernibly and then quickly regained its speed as it roared northward away from town. Lillie turned toward Kay to make a comment about foolish drivers but, with the sight of the child's face, held her tongue. The dark eyes, filled with fright, stood in stark contrast to the ashen features.

"What's the matter, Kay?"

"That car . . . I know that car," came the halting voice.

Lillie looked at her quizzically as Kay's eyes grew larger. The sound of the powerful engine was growing again as the vehicle, now southbound, neared the house. Kay sprang from her chair and ran to the front window, with Lillie rushing after her. The black Chevrolet Camaro turned into the driveway and lurched to a stop. Lillie felt both of the child's hands wrap around her left arm as the whimpers of fear grew in her throat.

"It's my uncle! Oh, God! It's my uncle. He said he'd get me the night they took Daddy away. Oh, God!"

Lillie quickly reached for the dead bolt latch on the front door; the metallic click shot through the room. She had only seconds, and her brain spun as the proper battle plan formed. She took Kay by both shoulders and stooped to look directly into her eyes.

"Do exactly as I say, girl, and do it now. There's a phone by my bed. Pick it up and punch nine-one-one, and say 'Trouble at Crow House. Come now.' Just say that, then stay in the room. Nine-one-one. Now go!"

Kay pounded up the steps as Lillie raced to the kitchen and snatched the electrical cord of the waffle iron from the plug. The baby played blissfully in the corner. Well fed and content, she would not move from her favorite spot. The gleeful sounds of the boys romping in the back yard were welcome. They would be safe there. Heavy footsteps pounded the wooden porch floor, followed by a violent rattling of the doorknob. As the first kick slammed against the door, Lillie snatched open a drawer and curled her fingers around a stainless steel knife with a six-inch blade. Ten feet separated her from the front door when the third kick sent it swinging wildly on its hinges.

Lillie felt a slight shudder pass through her body as she stared into the red-rimmed eyes of the man. He was not tall, but the bulk of his body filled the width of the doorway. Greasy black hair fell over his forehead, and his mouth was contorted into an ugly snarl. The pungent odor of alcohol and sweat drifted toward her as she fought the impulse to gag. He returned her stare for an eternal moment before speaking. The voice was raspy and venomous.

"I come for the lying little tramp, and I ain't leaving without her, old woman. I know she's in here."

"This is a home for children," Lillie said with all the calm she could muster, "and you cannot force your way in, and you won't be taking anyone without my permission."

"I been up all night wooling this thing over, and it ain't right. My brother's laid up in jail all on account of her lying mouth, and I mean to straighten her out. Send her on out here, now!"

"You're too late, mister, the Division of Family Services took her away last night."

"You're lying, old woman. My wife's done some

checking around. She's here all right. You send her out here, or I'll go find her myself! I ain't going to stand here and jaw all day!"

He took two steps forward before Lillie raised the knife that had been hidden behind her wrist. He halted in mid-stride and cocked his head at the gleaming blade. A crooked smile formed on his lips as he wheezed in soft laughter.

"My, my, but you're a feisty old bag, ain't you? I've a good mind to take that thing and mark you some on account of your bad manners. You throw that . . ."

"Shut up, you foul-mouthed crud, and listen to me," she hissed. "You're stronger than I am, but I've got the knife, and I swear to you, before it's over, I'll find a way to stick it in your gut and twist it."

The man blinked deliberately to clear his vision and looked into her eyes for signs of weakness or bluff, but there were none. For the first time he took note of her size, and his eyes fell to her bare forearm, the long muscles contracted and motionless. He swallowed against the dryness in his throat, and Lillie could see that he was recalculating the odds on having his way. Her ears strained for the sound of the sirens. Had Kay panicked and forgotten the number? Had her fears consumed her as she listened to the front door crashing open?

Sweet relief flooded through her as the distant sound pierced the morning. The man turned his head toward the door, and when he recognized the sound, looked back to Lillie in bewilderment.

STEVEN W. WISE   [45]

"You didn't do so well against the knife, big man. How will you do against the guns?" she snarled.

The dark eyes grew cloudy as the situation, now completely beyond his control, overwhelmed him. The snarl was gone from his mouth, now half open as he struggled to form words that would not come. The huge fists relaxed and thick fingers wiped nervously at the front of his trousers. He turned and took a quick step through the doorway only to see the first black and white cruiser screech to a halt behind his car. The second was coming into view on Morningside Road. The officer approached the porch at a half trot, his right hand on the grip of the revolver in its holster.

"You!" he commanded, pointing with his left forefinger at the intruder. "Off the porch! Now!"

The shaken man complied on unsteady legs and offered no resistance as the second officer approached, a nightstick in his hand. Still grimly clutching the knife, Lillie stepped out of the house and surveyed the unreal scene in the front yard.

"Ma'am, is everybody all right?" the older of the two policemen asked urgently.

"Everyone is fine, officer," came the steady reply. "This man kicked in our front door and threatened me and one of my children."

"Check out his car, Charlie."

Half of the younger man's body disappeared inside the vehicle and within seconds he emerged with the long barrel of a nickel-plated revolver in his hand.

MIDNIGHT

"It was under the driver's seat, Ross."

"Cuff this guy and get him in my car, will you?" He turned back to Lillie, whose eyes were still riveted on her antagonist. "Ma'am, I'm going to get a clipboard and a pad for your statement." He paused before continuing. "I believe it'll be okay now to put away the knife," he said with an easy smile.

Lillie's head jerked downward to her right hand and she looked up sheepishly. "Yes . . . yes, I suppose I ought to do that. I'll check on my other children and be right back."

She replaced the knife in the kitchen drawer and glanced down at the baby who had remained content in her mound of plastic. The faces of the twins were pressed against the top of the back door, their noses making tiny round blots on the glass. She opened the door and gently urged them back to their play.

"A bad driver out on the road, boys," she explained. "A couple of policemen stopped him to tell him about not driving so fast. Go on now, don't waste any more of this fine day."

When Lillie opened the bedroom door, Kay was sitting on the edge of the bed, both hands knotted tightly in her lap. Lillie sat down next to her and put an arm around her shoulder.

"Calm down, child. It's over. He was drunk. More mouth than anything else."

"No use trying to fool me, Miss Lillie. I know him better than you. He's got an awful mean streak.

I can't believe he didn't come for me. What did you say to him?"

"Well, I . . . I just tried to talk some sense to him, child, and anyway, you did such a good job with the call, the police were here in no time."

"I'm still shaking, Miss Lillie."

"Well, we can fix that. After I talk to this policeman for a few minutes, we're going to heat the waffle iron back up and finish breakfast. Don't suppose you'd put a dab of milk in the batter and beat it back up for us, would you?"

Kay drew in a long, ragged breath and felt the tension ease in her shoulders and arms. They arose as one from the bed and Lillie held her hand as they descended the stairs.

Five minutes later, the senior officer approached his vehicle and opened the door. He looked at his partner who was standing beside his own car, and the younger man chuckled with bemusement.

"Who'd we rescue, Ross, the old woman or the bad guy?"

Ross paused for a moment as he studied the big two-story house.

"My guess is that this bum was about to get his belly button relocated."

"Yeah. That's how I got it figured, too."

The car doors snapped shut in unison, and soon the only vehicle in the driveway was the shiny black Camaro. Thirty minutes later, a tow truck arrived and secured it to the long cable which hoisted the rear wheels off the pavement. The protector of

Crow House observed from the front porch as the undignified retreat down Morningside Road began.

◆

Two hours before dawn, Lillie awoke from a dreamless sleep with the vague feeling that she was not alone in the bedroom. Her first thought was that Kay, or possibly one of the twins, had come into the room, but the presence was much greater than that—unidentifiable yet powerful—and her unease grew by the moment. And then the thing vanished, and with it her discomfort, and she chided herself for allowing childlike thoughts to disturb her. She tossed about for a moment, drawing the pillow comfortably under her head, and sleep again claimed her.

The tumor in her breast boiled with activity—it was now the size of a marble—but even more diabolical was the insidious commotion within her brain. The dark invaders had sought and found the woman's bloodstream three months ago, and had traveled to her cerebrum. The delicate tissue had begun to succumb to the incessant onslaught, and her thought process, the very essence of her being, would soon be altered by the fallen angel's legion.

4

THE SOLITARY figure stood motionless among the hickory and oak trees that reached into the twilight. From his vantage point, twenty feet from the edge of a cliff overlooking the Missouri River, Carl Whittenburg studied the shadowy waters two hundred feet below as they swept endlessly past the town of Weston. The scratchy sounds of tiny night creatures filled his ears, and the gathering breeze carried an offering of meaty barbecue smoke from the town square a quarter mile south. Within the hour, a kaleidoscopic display of fireworks would illuminate the darkness and gigantic, flickering sparks would descend like meteorites seeking the river, only to perish in the air.

The earliest Fourth of July celebration Carl could remember took place in the same square seventy years before. He had been a part of it then, in tow with his two older brothers and proud parents, and it was a great celebration to be sure. The war to end all wars had just been fought and won, and the celebrants, cocksure in the knowledge that peace would be everlasting, reveled in the pride of it all. Then, Adolph Hitler was an unknown name in an unknown land, the sands of Iwo Jima were undefiled with blood, and young men would fall to the bullet and the bayonet no more.

The old man smiled ruefully as he thought of the seventy years since that had fashioned his life, and the lives of other sojourners on earth. It had been a long time since the small band of Pentecostals had been a part of the community. And now he *was* the small band, and the old church building was but a memory. Soon his bones would rest in the sea of stones at the east edge of town. But the thought of death to this life was no cause for trepidation in his heart. He looked down at the swift waters below and knew that even they would be consumed on that mighty day, but that he would not be.

He had walked among the tombstones earlier in the day and gathered strength from the memories of his parents and his brothers and Miss Hattie. In truth, like Saint Paul in the Bible, he longed to join them. To die was to gain; there was victory in death. But the victory would be postponed, of this he was sure. His thoughts turned to the old cloth in his top dresser drawer and to the woman who stood in need of it, wherever she was. It had been over two months and the Spirit had given him no direction, but he wasn't concerned. Long ago he had learned patience in dealing with the Spirit. At the proper time his prayers would be answered, and he would begin his journey. He would know when the time came.

The first missile whined into the night sky, bursting in embers of green and red which bathed the center of town in a dreamlike glow. And the crowd cheered and applauded, but some wept silently for loved ones lost to the three wars fought since the war to end all wars.

Another week passed before Carl knew it was time to begin his journey. The visitation took place late in the evening as the cottony breeze swirled about him on the front porch. His eyelids were heavy as he scolded himself for sitting in the metal chair until his body had stiffened. As he leaned forward to free himself from the chair, the sound of heavy, beating wings nearby froze him in place. He slowly eased his back against the chair and turned his head in the direction of the sound. He squinted into the moonlit yard for several seconds before he discerned the form of a large bird moving steadily toward him. Its stiff-legged gait and lurching motion were familiar sights to the man, but never before at this hour nor at this distance. It made no sound in the grass as it grew nearer still to the porch. Then, with an effortless flap of the long wings, it was on the porch, not more than eight feet from Carl. Surely something was wrong with the bird, he thought, as he watched the strange spectacle in amazement. He had never fed any bird purposely, least of all a crow, nor was he in the habit of leaving food scraps on the porch which might attract the irritating creatures. He stamped his foot and waved a hand at the bird.

"Get on out of here, you crazy fool!"

But it did not move, and as Carl looked into the beady eyes that would not leave his, he felt the goose flesh begin at the base of his neck and crawl down his back. He could not take his eyes off the crow, and only after an interminable ten seconds did the bird turn and strut to the edge of the porch, its clawed feet making faint clicking noises on the wood floor. Then it swiveled its head to the man, as if to see that he was still watching, and took to the night air. Carl clambered from his chair and quickly stepped into the yard. With powerful strokes of its wings, the crow flew on an unwavering line, and in the sheen of light, the man watched until it became a speck, and then disappeared.

"East by southeast," Carl whispered. "And she lives far away."

It took him ten minutes to find the old telephone book in a disorderly heap of magazines and worn books. It had been five years since a telephone was in the house, but he remembered he had kept the directory, and he remembered that an area code map of the States was in it somewhere. He leafed through only six pages behind the front cover before finding it. He rummaged through a drawer in the kitchen and pulled out a pencil with which he made a heavy dot at a place he reckoned to be

Weston—on the Missouri-Kansas border near the point where the boundary turned northwest. He laid the pencil under the mark with the point due east and began to sweep slowly to the south. The dull tip passed through Virginia and he knew that could not be the state; even the southern region was almost due east of Weston, and the bird had clearly flown to the southeast. But the Carolinas were southeast, and so was Georgia and Florida, and they all stretched to the great Atlantic, as far away as a man could go. His rough fingertip grated on the thin paper as it traversed the four states from north to south, and then back up the coast. She was there; he knew with a certainty that could not be denied and his spine tingled with the thought. He studied the map again and covered the area which was barely over two finger widths long on the paper, but which touched, he calculated, a thousand miles of the earth. He was not disheartened with the knowledge, and tomorrow, when the library doors opened, he would be there, and he assured himself that before noon he would have a list of cities and towns along the coast. And then he would continue to watch, and wait, and trust.

The lady at the library was helpful, and after Carl made his needs known, she led him to a section of shelves which offered materials on geography. Fifteen minutes later he shuffled wearily into the house with the large book tucked under his arm. After a drink of cool water, he cleared the kitchen table and opened the book, carefully folding out the map of the United States. Using the handle of a long wooden spoon as a straight edge, he held the left end over Weston and nudged the tip of the handle downward with his right forefinger. He chewed on his lower lip thoughtfully as a steady progression of names popped out from under his fingertip. He pushed away from the table and walked out of the house and into the front yard. The morning was heavy with the promise of a stifling day, and the breeze made a half-hearted effort at stirring the tree branches overhead. He moved a step to the spot from which he saw the crow depart the night before.

"Lord, Lord, there's a heap of towns down that way, a heap of them," he whispered to the sky. "I'm not getting any younger and the woman—she isn't getting any better."

He shook his head slowly and turned to go back inside when the softly spoken words of his mother echoed in his head from sixty years in the past, the scene unfolding in dreamlike fashion. He had overheard her counsel a friend who lamented the lack of direction given to her by the Spirit. The words rang in his ears with the same urgency conveyed so long ago.

"Esther, we are given direction every step of the way, but the Spirit is not going to beat us over the head. Chances are He has already pointed you, but you don't trust enough to take action."

He squinted again at the line the crow had flown; he had marked it with the chimney of a neighbor's house. The street was laid out on a perfect east-west axis. He raised his right arm parallel with it, and then pointed to the chimney, taking careful note of the angle formed. Purposeful strides took him back to the kitchen where he found a pencil and sat down at the table. The spoon handle was replaced over Weston and as his brow furrowed with the effort, he attempted to duplicate the angle on the map. Once satisfied that he had done his best, he drew a faint line along the last two inches of the handle and then withdrew it to study the result. The end of the line touched the long finger of Pamlico Sound as it jutted into land, but first it had passed through the center of a tiny, open circle that represented a town—the last town before the great ocean. And within the circle, thousands of inhabitants went about the business of life in Washington, North Carolina.

He eased his back against the hard chair and passed his hand between the two unruly shocks of hair. The woman he sought was there. He knew.

At ten minutes after nine the next morning, Carl walked through the front door of Weston State Bank with three hundred and seventeen dollars— the balance of his checking and savings accounts, less minimum deposits. He walked two blocks south to Bestgen's Store, which also doubled as the town bus depot. The proprietress loomed in disarray behind the dirty counter.

"Morning," Carl said as he approached the counter.

"Morning to you. What you need?"

"A bus ticket to Washington, North Carolina."

"Good Lord. Never heard of the place."

Carl waited patiently as Ada Bestgen fumbled through a sheaf of papers held together by a single staple.

"Looks like it's going to run you ninety-nine bucks plus tax one way, Carl. Leaves at eight in the morning. Long ways down there, you know. Got relatives?"

"No. Just a friend," Carl replied with a smile. He pulled his wallet from his hip pocket and counted out two fifties and a ten and handed them to the woman. Carl calculated his finances while Ada made change for the ten dollar bill. Deducting the fare back home, he would have a little over one hundred dollars with which to eat and sleep. It would suffice, he assured himself. A way to the woman would be provided without undue delay. Had not the Spirit already proven Himself, yet again, with the crow? He had checked with the bank teller about having his next Social Security deposit wired to him if necessary. It would come in eight days, but he was confident that he would not need it.

Ada counted the four one dollar bills over the ticket and banged the loose coins over them with a puffy hand.

"You know it's going to take you at least thirty-six rotten hours to get there don't you? The bus folks

STEVEN W. WISE   [57]

would kill me if they could hear me talking like that, but I want folks to know what they're getting into. I took a long bus ride once myself. Lord, have mercy! When the last leg was over, the driver and another strong man had to haul my carcass out of that seat. Came back on a jet plane to Kansas City, I did. Cost more, but great day, it was worth every cent."

"Thanks for the warning, Ada, but I aim to fly only once in my life, and it isn't going to be in a metal tube."

The big woman looked quizzically at him as he threw up his hand in a friendly wave of goodbye and turned to the door.

He returned to his house and went directly to the cluttered closet in the spare bedroom. The musty odor of things long unused filled his nostrils as he rummaged for the battered suitcase. He would wear his best dark slacks and one of the three short-sleeved dress shirts. The other two were carefully folded and placed in the suitcase along with under-wear, socks, handkerchiefs, and the threadbare jacket which carried the name of his last employer on its back. He ran his fingers over the faint letter-ing that spelled "Hunt Concrete."

"Ten years since I finished any mud," he mum-bled, using the concrete worker's favorite nickname for the unruly material.

He picked up the frame of cloth and the Bible and gently placed them in the bottom of a heavy paper sack, folding the excess paper tightly around the objects. He secured the sack with two strands of thin twine and then hefted the parcel in his hands to check for sturdiness. Satisfied, he tucked it into the suitcase and buffered it with the underwear and socks. His toilet kit would be added after his morning bath. He could think of nothing else of importance that he might need, and as he looked over the contents of the suitcase, he felt that the only two things he really needed were wrapped in the brown grocery sack.

◆

From his seat ten rows back on the right side of the bus, Carl observed the mid-Missouri landscape as it swept lazily by. After a short lunch stop on the western fringe of St. Louis, the cumbersome vehicle labored back onto Interstate 70 and slowly regained cruising speed. Soon the lush countryside was displaced by concrete and glaring panes of tinted glass. Then, as the core of the great city loomed to the right, the brown monotony of slovenly industrial buildings became a backdrop for shabby row housing, the inhabitants milling on front porches in search of a comforting breeze.

The brown package rested securely in Carl's lap, the fingers of his left hand toying with the taut strings. When the driver had insisted the small suitcase be placed in the baggage compartment, Carl had patiently laid it on the sidewalk and retrieved the precious package before relinquishing the tattered piece of luggage to the belly of the metal beast.

Two passengers departed the bus in East St. Louis, Illinois, and one climbed aboard, and then the bus continued on down Interstate 64 as its massive wheels consumed the pavement leading to Mt. Vernon and another stop. The afternoon sunlight warmed the side of Carl's face for an hour as they rolled south on Interstate 57, then it was gone as Interstate 24 stretched to the southeast and the Kentucky border. Mile after endless mile, the diesel engine droned, steady and unburdened over the flat terrain as it propelled the bus toward Paducah, Kentucky, and the death of seven passengers.

It was over within five horrifying seconds. The last sounds Carl heard were the screeching of tires and a wailing chorus of fear as he felt the bus pitch wildly to the left and then down the embankment. The black void and the silence came simultaneously.

◆

The world came back in hazy patches of light and shadows, and the voice of a woman, faraway and soothing, touched his ears.

"Mr. Whittenburg . . . Mr. Whittenburg. Can you hear me now?"

As he tried to turn toward the sound, daggers of pain paralyzed his head and neck and suddenly every fiber of his body was alive and on fire. He fought to clear his mind and forced himself to move his head an agonizing inch to the left as the voice spoke again, clearer this time.

"You're all right, Mr. Whittenburg. You're going to be all right. You've got a broken leg and a lot of bumps and bruises, but you'll be okay soon. Don't worry."

The white uniform hovering over him slowly came into focus and he remembered the cries of the passengers in the bus. His hands clenched at his sides for the brown paper parcel, and a feeling of dread crept over him. His mouth was dry and his tongue would barely function as he attempted to speak.

"Did . . . did they find my . . . package . . . in the bus?"

"I don't know, Mr. Whittenburg, but I know they did recover most of the baggage from the wreckage."

"Don't care . . . about that . . . just the package."

"I'll have someone call the bus company. Don't worry about that for now. Just get some rest." She patted his hand gently and checked the intravenous line and the tape holding the needle in place. "I'm going to put some medicine in your I.V., Mr. Whittenburg. It'll help you rest. Okay?"

His strength was waning and the pain was a prickly blanket over his body, but he struggled to speak once more.

"You call . . . soon . . . please. It didn't look

STEVEN W. WISE

like much. . . just a paper sack . . . wrapped tight with string. . . ."

"I promise. It's been over three hours since the wreck. I'm sure they've taken care of everything."

"Did anybody . . . die . . . in it?"

"I'm afraid so. There were seven that didn't make it. You were very lucky."

♦

The receptionist glanced up from her work and studied the tall man as he entered the hospital lobby. He moved with a grace that belied his size and quickly approached the desk. He wore the faded denim coveralls of a farmer and a long-sleeved white shirt that was much nicer than the outer garment. His expansive face was framed by thick white hair, worn long, that caught the fluorescent light from the ceiling fixture in an eerie glow.

As the young woman looked up into the purest blue eyes she had ever seen, she stumbled over the words she had spoken hundreds of times.

"Er . . . ah . . . how can I . . . I help you, sir?"

The man extended his right hand and placed a small string-bound package of brown paper on the desk. His voice was resonant and forceful, yet unthreatening.

"Would you kindly see that this package is returned to Carl Whittenburg? He was in the bus accident this evening."

"Well . . . yes, sir, I will. . . . If you're sure it belongs to a patient of ours. We were told that the highway patrol and the bus company people had taken care of all personal belongings in the wreckage."

The trace of a smile crossed his lips as he nodded. "Yes, I know. But this was overlooked."

She carefully inspected the package for any sign of identification, but the paper was unmarked.

"Well . . . I don't know how you can be sure this belongs to a certain person if there's no . . ."

"I rewrapped my friend's Bible."

"Yes . . . well . . . let me get this straight. You came up on this wreck scene, and a . . . friend of yours happened to be a victim, and you found his . . ."

He raised his right hand ever so slightly, but the motion silenced her. "I was with him on the bus," he said.

The woman's brow furrowed as she looked into the incredible blue eyes again, but she could not hold his gaze. As she lowered her head, her eyes swept over his body in search of wounds or bandages. She remembered how he had approached her desk. He had not walked like a man just hours removed from a horrible bus accident.

"I was very fortunate not to have been harmed." He paused, smiling warmly, and she looked up long enough to see the smile. "I will trust you to see that the Bible is returned to Mr. Whittenburg."

Without another word, he turned and left the

STEVEN W. WISE   [63]

lobby. The receptionist shook her head quizzically for a moment as she hefted the package in her hands, inspected it for any sign of identification, and then laid it in front of her. She flipped through the patient register, running her finger down the listing of names until it stopped abruptly. The telephone was cradled expertly between her ear and shoulder as she peeled a page from a small yellow pad and printed the name and room number on it.

"Yes, this is Ruby down at the front desk. Send an orderly down here, will you? Some . . . ah . . . person just brought in a package for one of the bus wrecks."

Cathy Hatfield smiled to herself as she carried the package down the hallway toward Room 206. She had just found time to make some telephone calls for the old man when the object he sought was hand-delivered to her.

"Double lucky, old fellow," she whispered as she placed the package on the top shelf of the small closet near his bed.

It was noon the next day before Carl woke completely and felt anxiety over the missing cloth return. At his first opportunity, he questioned the day nurse about the sack, but she seemed harried and showed little inclination to pursue the matter. She gently but firmly informed him that the evening shift nurse would come on duty in less than three hours, and that she would have more time to devote to his non-medical needs.

At two forty-five, Cathy arrived on the floor and entered the nurses' conference room, where the nurses going off duty would report on patient conditions to the new shift. As usual the dialogue was brief and to the point, covering medications, doctors' instructions, and any special patient problems. Cathy listened attentively and jotted notes as Nina Wilbert went down the list of patients on her wing.

"Mr. Whittenburg seems to be doing fine. Slept all morning. Didn't ask for pain medication one time. Just bugged me about some package he lost on the bus. He said you promised to call and check on it for . . ."

"It's on the shelf in his closet," Cathy interjected. "Didn't Bonnie tell you at report this morning? They brought it up last night."

"No. She must have forgotten, I guess. I wish I had known. He seemed overly concerned. Oh, well, you've got it made with him now. No problems."

The meeting broke up in a few minutes, and Cathy walked briskly to Room 206.

"Hi there, Mr. Whittenburg. I hear you haven't heard the good news yet."

His eyes followed her as she walked directly to the closet and opened the door. When he saw the sack in her hands, he sighed with relief and spoke fervently, more in direct address than in prayer, to an unseen God.

"Oh yes! Lord God Almighty . . . Oh yes! Forgive me for doubting the power of Your hand."

Cathy was surprised by the conviction in the old

man's voice; there was a power in it that should not have belonged to him, an aged accident victim, but it was there, unmistakable, nearly palpable in the close air of the room. She handed him the sack and he accepted it with both hands as if he were receiving a prize beyond measure.

"Someone from the bus company must have brought it to you, Mr. Whittenburg," and as she said the words, Cathy again let her eyes fall on the package. She had seen no mark of identification last night, but she had only glanced at it; now she had seen it twice, and she was sure there was no mark to be seen. They must have opened it, found the name, and re-tied the string; of course, she thought, that was exactly what had happened. There was simply no other explanation.

His eyes were closed now and she could trace the glint of a tear as it slid toward his right temple. She started to speak but the words caught on her tongue, and she left the room quietly.

When his prayer was finished, he pushed at the strings with his fingertips and inspected the same knots that he had tied in his bedroom the night before. In his life he had tied everything from fishing line to thick rope and his knots were unfailingly precise. No one had re-tied the strings; of this he was certain. He brought the sack to his mouth and bit through the strands one by one. The heavy paper crackled open and he cautiously inserted his hand, feeling for the shards of glass that would surely be there. His fingers touched the coarseness of the Bible cover and then the smooth glass covering the cloth. He took it from the sack and when he saw the small pane was unbroken, he knew as surely as he knew life that he did not journey alone. The glass appeared to be pristine and was without a single flaw.

Over the next four days, the pulsing throb in his leg ebbed along with the aches that were scattered mainly along the right side of his body. He reasoned that he must have been thrown on that side when the bus crashed. The stitches in the hairline of his brow began to itch, and he knew this was a normal sign of healing. His vision cleared up nicely and his appetite returned with a vengeance. The hospital fare was palatable, if unexciting, and he knew it was nourishing. Every tray was taken from his room without a speck of food remaining, and he took a considerable amount of good-natured ribbing from kitchen workers who were used to hearing complaints about the food. His quiet demeanor and courtesy quickly endeared him to the staff, especially to Cathy. In the fourth month of her initial staff assignment, she was having some difficulty dealing with the unreasonable moans and groans of a surprising number of patients who seemingly felt they were each the sole reason for her employment. The only difficulty she encountered with Carl was in convincing him that his hospital bill was of no concern; the bus company was bound to have insurance, and if that were not enough, the hospital provided indigent care. Their conversations lasted only a few minutes at a time, but a bond had formed between the grandfatherly gentleman and the young woman. And they were both comfortable in the knowledge of it.

The supper tray was being taken from his room when Cathy passed by the kitchen assistant in the doorway. She was a portly woman with a round face set off by mischievous eyes that seemed to rest on cheeks made garish by an over-zealous application of rouge.

"Watch out, missy. This old man will bite your hand off if you get it too close to his mouth." She howled with delight as Carl feigned indignity at the statement and waved a hand in her direction.

"I wish all of my patients ate like you," Cathy said. "They'd get their strength back a lot sooner—just like you have." Cathy moved to his bedside and prepared to change the dressing on his head wound.

"Nice having someone around who can appreciate a good appetite," Carl said as he smiled a greeting.

He studied her face as she went about her task with practiced ease. It was a winsome face—a perfect match for her personality. Her starched, white cap stood in contrast with the inky waves of hair supporting it. Her complexion was fair, unusually so Carl thought, for the owner of hair so black. The green eyes were deeply set and warm as they darted downward every few moments to check Carl's face for signs of discomfort. Her lips were full and parted easily over prominent teeth, the top middle two overlapping slightly to form the only imperfection in the oval face.

She was slight in stature, standing barely five feet by Carl's guess. Her eyes were not much above his as he sat propped forward in the bed. She quickly replaced the old dressing with a fresh one, gathered the discarded bandages, and dropped her scissors in the front pocket of her uniform.

"That will do it, Mr. Whittenburg. Looks good, real good. You're some kind of a quick healer, you know?"

"Must be all this good attention I get," he replied as Cathy stepped to the door. "Oh, child, one more thing. 'Mr. Whittenburg' is an awful mouthful. 'Carl' suits me just fine."

Cathy smiled and nodded deferentially. "Carl it is."

She moved with the energy of youth, her pointed cap bobbing up and down in snappy cadence as she left the room. He smiled to himself and knew that he would truly miss her. But he could not stay in the hospital any longer than absolutely necessary. Without the knowledge that he was being attended by powers greater than man, the decision to proceed east or return home to heal would have required considerable thought. But the power, in whatever form, was with him, always nearby. As soon as he could get on crutches he intended to be on his way.

By ten o'clock, Cathy had attended to the needs

of all her patients; the transition to the night shift would be smooth and orderly. She had worked steadily without a break since coming on the floor in order to save a few minutes to visit with Carl. Religion had never been of any real interest to her, except for the well-publicized escapades of television evangelists. Those scandals convinced her that whatever they had was obviously not worth seeking. Yet this quiet old man, whose silent prayers and kind actions seemed so real, so uncontrived, had drawn her to him without so much as one direct word about God.

She tapped lightly on the open door as she walked into his room. He was propped up in his favorite position, with the night lamp casting a subdued light over his shoulder on the objects in his lap. She hesitated when she saw the empty paper sack and the old book resting beside it. A smaller object was nearly lost in his hands. Although her curiosity had grown over the past few days, she had not inquired about the contents of the precious sack. Now, she had managed to blunder into the only semblance of privacy the old man owned, and she could not hide her dismay. Carl immediately saw her dilemma and eased her discomfort.

"Come over and pull up a chair, child. I was hoping you'd come by to say good night."

"Carl, I . . . didn't mean to . . ."

"Hush, child. I meant what I just said."

He motioned for her to come to his bedside and

she complied, pulling the chair forward as he directed with slight waves of his hand.

"High time I shared these things with you, it is for a fact, girl. Wouldn't do it with just anybody. Only a friend." He smiled reassuringly and Cathy managed a weak smile in return.

"This was my mother's Bible," he said as he held it out for her to accept. "Thought it was lost until a few months ago. It and this cloth." He passed the small frame to her.

Cathy slowly turned the frame in her hand, inspecting the precision of the joints and the tight backing.

"I've never seen a piece of cloth framed before," she said.

"It was my mother's too. Only she and one other woman knew where it came from, and they never told anyone. Momma and Miss Hattie, both gone now—Miss Hattie only a few months ago—used it to show sick people about faith. I reckon that now you'd call them faith healers."

He paused, looking at her face for a reaction, and thought he noticed a hint of unease.

"I know it sounds strange, Cathy, but I was there, and I saw the power of it over and over again. Not the power of Momma and Miss Hattie, mind you, or any power in this here piece of cloth, but the power of Christ. They had the gift of showing the sick the power of Christ, the same power as two thousand years ago. Then, a woman in the crowd was healed just by touching His garment as he passed by, so great was her faith. Momma loved that scripture in the book of Mark. She said there's no less of His power today than long ago. It's just that people won't trust in it."

"I don't know much about the Bible, Carl," she said apologetically. "Religion has never seemed to offer much for me. Seems like I know more good people without it than with it. Don't misunderstand, I'm not disputing anything you say, it's just . . ."

"Don't mix up religion with Christ, child. Hitler had religion, but he sure didn't have Christ!"

She nodded without speaking and ran her finger around the edge of the frame. "So, where are you headed with these things?"

"Place in North Carolina. Town called Washington."

"You're going to try and help a friend?"

"Yes . . . you could say that. She . . . is a friend. I mean to get back on the road soon, too."

"She'll understand, I'm sure. You've called her, haven't you?"

Carl paused and passed a hand through the wild shock of hair on the side of his head. "Well . . . I . . . well, the truth is, child, I don't know exactly who she is, I just know she's there."

"How in the world do you know that?" Cathy asked, barely able to keep the incredulity in her voice at an acceptable level.

"I'm led by powers far greater than me, Cathy. I can't explain it to you. I just know."

She shook her head slowly and placed the frame

on the Bible before handing it back to Carl. She looked directly into his eyes and he held her gaze.

"Carl, if there wasn't something about you that I can't put my finger on, I swear I'd tell your doctor you need a shrink."

He chuckled softly and reached for the sack. "You'll probably go home and tell your husband you've got a crazy old man to entertain you."

She stood to leave and patted his hand in parting. "No, Carl Whittenburg, I'll tell him I've got a mysterious, elderly gentleman under my care who's on a strange mission. How's that?"

"Ha! I'll bet that's what you'll tell him," he laughed.

"I promise, Carl. Mysterious, not crazy," she said as she neared the doorway.

"Remember now, child. Hitler had religion."

She shook her head once more before disappearing into the hallway.

◆

It was fifteen minutes before midnight when the electrical hum of the garage door opener disturbed Kevin Hatfield's light slumber. Although he arose at six o'clock, he never allowed himself sound sleep until Cathy was safely home from her shift. The sound of laughter from Johnny Carson's audience filled the small bedroom as she bounced through the doorway.

STEVEN W. WISE   [73]

"Hi, babe," she said, checking for his state of drowsiness.

"Hi, Cat. How was your shift?"

"Good, except for one fat-bottomed broken leg that refuses to use what few muscles she has in her body. I feel like I've wrestled a perfumed bear when I leave her room."

Kevin chuckled at her answer. "Now that doesn't sound like Florence Nightingale to me."

"Florence would have said the same thing if she'd had this old gal to tug on all night."

She plopped down beside him on the bed, kicked off her shoes, and sighed luxuriously, making a tight circle with her lips as her cheeks puffed slightly. Kevin rolled over and laid his head on her shoulder, draping his arm over her waist.

"How's your old friend with the strange sack doing?"

"Strong as a horse. He ought to be discharged with crutches in a couple of days. I found out what was in the sack tonight. Didn't mean to. I went in his room to talk for a few minutes at the end of the shift, and he had it on his lap. I was going to leave, but he practically made me stay."

"Well, what the dickens was in it?"

"Just a beat-up old Bible that belonged to his mother and a little piece of cloth in a frame."

"That was it?"

"Yes, that was it. But after he told me the story behind them . . . I . . . well, I can see how they would be precious to an old man."

"His mother's Bible maybe, but what's with the cloth?"

"He said his mother was a faith healer years ago . . ."

"Aw, no . . ."

"Wait a minute and let me finish, you big lunk. There's a story somewhere in the Bible about a sick woman who healed herself by touching Jesus' clothes or something. It's got something to do with that."

Kevin groaned.

"What's really interesting is that he's on his way to North Carolina to help some woman he doesn't even know yet."

"What do you mean 'yet'? He knows her name and where she lives. How can he not know her 'yet'?"

"He doesn't know her name, or exactly where she lives. He says he just knows she's in a certain town and needs help."

"This poor old fellow's got a head wound y'all haven't found yet, that's what I think."

"I know it sounds goofy. But I swear, this man is *not* a kook. There's something about him that's just . . . just real. Why would he make up a story like that?"

"Why does any senile old person say things that don't make sense?"

"Kevin Hatfield, you're about to make me mad. I'm telling you, I've been around sick, old brains before, and there isn't anything wrong with Carl."

STEVEN W. WISE   [75]

"Whatever, nurse. I give up. I need to get a little sleep." He rolled over, gathered the sheet, and burrowed his head into the pillow.

"He thinks he's ready to hit the road, crutches and all, but he's not. I'm going to try and talk him into going back home to recuperate, but if he won't do that, I'll try to help him find a cheap room here for a while."

"Does he have any money?"

"He says he has some and that he can have his social security checks sent to him if he needs to."

"Whatever," came the muffled voice from the pillow. "Just don't get too wrapped up in this. Okay?"

There was no reply as a click silenced the laughter from the television. The last sound Kevin heard before he slept was soft footsteps on the carpet.

Over the next three days, Cathy and the attending physician were able to convince Carl that he should allow himself a reasonable recuperation period after being discharged from the hospital. In truth, he had acquiesced only because the urge to continue his journey had somehow abated. The Spirit had calmed him and given him rest. He would gather his strength for the final push to the east. Cathy had located a boarding house at the south edge of town. The operator agreed to provide room and board for sixty-five dollars a week.

Cathy arrived at the hospital on the morning of Carl's discharge to drive him to the boarding house. When she entered his room, he was leaning on his crutches, breathing heavily from the exertion of hobbling around the room.

"Look at you," she exclaimed from the doorway. "Getting the feel of those sticks, are you?"

"I think they're getting the feel of me, child," he said, shaking his head tiredly.

"Well, you'll have plenty of time to practice after we get you settled in your room. Everybody in this place gets a wheelchair ride when they leave, so sit down and relax for a minute while I get your things together."

An orderly popped into the room with a wheel-chair, and assisted Cathy in seating Carl.

"I'll drive," Cathy winked at the young man. He picked up the suitcase and the crutches. The paper sack, now bound with surgical tape, rested in Carl's lap.

The modest procession moved down the hall toward the elevator. As they neared the last room on the wing, the kitchen assistant with the rosy cheeks emerged from the doorway holding a half-eaten breakfast tray.

"Lord have mercy," she bellowed, "Carl's leaving us. I'm going to tell the boss to fire half the cooks. You take care, old buddy."

"The same to you, Beulah. I'll miss you," he replied.

"Lawdy, I'm sure you will, like a case of the flu," she cackled.

The ding of the elevator bell cut off the conversation, and within seconds, Carl and his attendants were consumed by the shiny, metal doors.

With Carl stretched across the back seat of her car, Cathy drove the quarter circle of driveway to the four-lane street and merged with the morning traffic.

"It's not too far, Carl. I'll get you cooled off back there in a minute."

"I'm fine, Cathy. I make do with a fan and shade trees at home."

The bright sunlight on the passing buildings was a drastic change from the artificial light of his hospital room and he squinted his eyes. He looked at the black hair jutting above the seat and felt a swell of tenderness for the young woman who had taken him under her wing.

"Child . . . I don't know how to thank you properly for helping me like this. But I do the best I can. I surely do."

"Don't worry about thanking me, Carl. I'm doing it because I want to. I'm glad I can help."

Neither spoke for several minutes as the din of the passing vehicles filled the car.

"Did you ever tell your husband what I'm trying to do?"

"Yes . . . I mentioned it to him the same night you showed me the Bible and cloth."

"Poor fellow. I imagine he thinks I'm a crazy old man."

"Well, he did wonder about it, but I straightened

him out. I told him there isn't anything wrong with your head!"

They laughed easily together.

"Someday I'll tell you how it all comes out down there."

"I'll hound you to the ends of the earth if you don't, Carl Whittenburg."

Cathy braked the car steadily to a halt on a tree-lined street. Carl looked intently at the old two-story frame house, sitting close to the curb. It was covered with asbestos shingle siding, the bulk of which appeared to be in good repair. The windows were large, with clean panes and shutters painted dark green. The covered porch with a scattering of metal and cloth-covered lawn chairs, ran across the front and wrapped around one side of the house. The tiny front lawn was neatly cut and a narrow concrete walk bisected it. Cathy retrieved Carl's suitcase and the sack from the front seat and placed them on the front porch before returning to assist him. There were four steps leading to the front porch.

"Steps are tricky, Carl," she warned, watching closely as he struggled with the unfamiliar crutches.

She tapped the door knocker and waited for the owner to appear. The front door swung open and a woman no taller than Cathy stood before them. She was dressed in a sleeveless cotton print dress covered by an apron. She was using the corner to dry her hands. Her face, framed by wisps of thin gray hair, was etched with lines, the kind carved by long years of exposure to sun and wind. But they did not detract from the warmth radiating from her eyes.

"You must be Mr. Whittenburg," she said, reaching for his right hand resting on the handle of the crutch. "No, don't let go, for heaven's sake," she said laughing. "I'll shake it proper when you sit down. I'm Mable Foster and I'm pleased to meet you."

"The pleasure's mine, ma'am," Carl said.

"And your name was . . . Katy?"

"Cathy, Mrs. Foster. Cathy Hatfield. I'm the one who called for Carl."

"I'm sorry, honey. You'd think a woman my age would have learned to remember names better by now." She turned back to Carl. "You come on in, Mr. Whittenburg . . ."

"Carl, please," he interjected softly.

"Carl it is then. Suits me fine, because I'm just Mable to everybody around here. Let's get you settled in. I have some fresh corn stewing and new potatoes, and the first decent tomatoes I've seen all season. We eat dinner early around here. Hope that's okay?"

"I'll eat anytime you ring the bell, Mable," Carl said with a smile.

"Missy, I can see me and your friend here are going to hit it off just fine."

Cathy patted Carl's hand in parting. "You've got my numbers, at work and at home, Carl. Just call for anything you need. I'll come and get you next week for your checkup if I don't see you sooner. Kevin's got one venison roast left from last fall, and we're saving it for you. Maybe I'll just take you home with me after your checkup. How's that sound?"

"That would be wonderful, child. I'll look forward to it."

She turned and danced down the porch steps two at a time as the two figures stood motionless, watching from the doorway.

"Lordy, Lordy, I used to move like that, but now I can't remember what it felt like," Mable said wistfully. "Mighty nice young lady, that's plain to see. You're lucky to have a friend like that."

Carl nodded and stood silently for a moment as he watched Cathy's car disappear down the street.

"More than luck, Mable," he said. "It's more than luck."

The woman held the screen door open as Carl awkwardly made his way into the house.

5

LILLIE AWOKE to the familiar clatter of the baby's bed rail as he pounded it against the wall of the adjacent bedroom. The quiet baby girl had been placed in a home the week before. The void created by her absence was quickly filled by the most active fifteen-month-old child Lillie had ever encountered. The boy was actually small for his age, but his tiny body was always in motion, as if charged with electricity. He required nearly constant attention during his waking hours, and it seemed he rarely slept. Lillie was thankful for Kay's assistance. The twins were still in Crow House, and the addition of another six-year-old boy created a threesome that exuded an energy level of considerable proportion in its own right.

Lillie swung her legs over the side of the bed and felt with her toes for her slippers. She was mildly irritated that the pain in her right breast had persisted into the third day since the baby bumped her.

She had leaned over to pick the child up when a typical burst of energy had propelled his head upward and directly into the side of her breast. The pain was surprisingly sharp, but no worse than that caused by hundreds of assorted bumps and gouges meted out over the years by lively residents. She stood before the mirror and made a half-hearted effort at straightening her hair.

"You're getting old, Lillie," she scolded the reflection. "Can't even take a bump from a baby."

When Lillie stuck her head through the doorway, Kay was already in the baby's room. She was holding the boy's hands in hers as he jumped up and down, pummeling the little mattress. High-pitched squeaks from the crib seemed a protest to the abuse. The child's red hair, concentrated in an unruly shock near the front of his head, waved like a tiny handkerchief. He squealed with glee, his open mouth revealing two gleaming dots of white protruding from his lower gums.

"Well, I see young Andrew is ready for the day," Lillie said.

"He's something else, ain't he?" Kay replied.

Lillie walked to the bed and took a tissue from her gown pocket. "Let's wipe up some of that slobber before you soak your p.j.'s, young man." She dabbed at the moving target with little success. He soon grew tired of the jumping game and Kay released his hands, allowing him to plop softly on the mattress. His eyes darted hopefully from Kay to Lillie in anticipation of the next game to be played.

STEVEN W. WISE   [83]

Lillie reached for his face with two fingers and stroked the faint bruises along his jaw line.

"About healed up, huh, baby? Doesn't hurt any more, does it?" Lillie cooed.

"You think he remembers?" Kay asked softly.

"No, honey, I doubt it. He just knows he's happy now. Babies just know the 'now' of life."

Lillie allowed her thoughts to drift back to the day baby Andrew had arrived from the hospital. His eyes bore no mischief that morning, only emptiness. As Lillie knew well, emptiness in a baby's eyes is a haunting thing, an unnatural thing. That had been the only time she had seen Susan Kelly cry openly. Lillie and Kay had wept unashamedly with her as they heard the story gush from Susan in sobs and sniffles. The boyfriend of the child's mother had committed the atrocity, dunking the baby repeatedly into the toilet bowl, head first and with force, for the crime of wetting the floor when he wasn't wearing his diaper. The "mother," and Susan had spat the word from her mouth, had finally managed to break the spell of rage and rescue her son, but not before his lungs were tainted with filthy water and not before his jaw was dislocated. But in the living room of Crow House, he was cleansed as the tears of two women and a child fell on his broken body, and the healing power of love began to infuse him as tender hands caressed his skin. The light in his eyes was returned to him.

"How about changing him while I start breakfast?" Lillie asked. "With any luck, I'll have it ready before the rest of the hounds start baying."

She first became aware of the darkness in her mind at bedtime. She had instructed the twins to begin their baths half an hour before, but they had persisted in a series of raucous games which had spilled out of their room into the hall. As she cleared the top step and advanced toward them, the need to separate them and proceed with the routine gave way to a nearly overpowering urge to strike them, not with an ordinary open-handed tap on their bottoms, but with clenched fists against their heads. As she reached the tangle of bodies, she realized with horror that her right fist was drawn above her head and aimed at one of the boys. But the feeling of rage passed in an instant, and her mind reeled as she reached for the railing to steady herself.

"My God. What . . . " she said aloud.

The twins had not noticed her action. Their attention was directed to the labor of untangling arms and legs. They sat up, puffing for breath and red-faced, and looked up at Lillie.

"You two . . . please . . . just get your baths. Okay?"

They bounced up and scrambled down the hallway in a race for the bathroom.

The voice from the bottom of the stairs was inquisitive and concerned. "You okay, Miss Lillie?"

"Yes . . . yes, Kay. I'm . . . just tired, I guess."

STEVEN W. WISE   [85]

Later, the Agatha Christie novel lay open beside her on the bed. The house was quiet, with only the soothing tick of the big clock in the hallway filling her ears. She had tried in vain to get into the narrative of the book, but the incident earlier in the evening would not leave her. The thought that she might have struck a child in anger was staggering—something as foreign to her life as hatred itself. And yet, she had actually drawn back her clenched fist. It was too much to contemplate.

She shook her head in bewilderment and marked the book before extending her right arm to place it on the nightstand. The stab of pain in her breast was followed by a hiss as she caught her breath. She reached instinctively with her left hand to the source of the pain. She probed cautiously with her fingertips at the tenderness. The pain should be going away, not growing worse, she told herself. Determined to discover what was wrong, she ignored the discomfort and continued to probe the area until the tip of her middle finger discovered the hardness of a knot. So that's it, she assured herself; the baby's head had struck her with enough force to cause the knotting of deep tissue. It was little wonder that the pain was intense and stubborn, especially considering that she had done nothing to promote any healing. She climbed out of bed and walked to the closet. After a few moments of searching, she felt the electrical cord of the heating pad, and pulled it from the shelf. With a damp

MIDNIGHT

washcloth placed under the pad, Lillie settled back into bed. She was confident that a little deep heat would soon take care of this bothersome ache, and possibly improve her disposition as well.

As the warmth from the heating pad began to creep over her, it soon masked enough of the pain that she felt drowsy. She clicked the control of the heating pad to off and then the light switch, before fluffing the pillow and settling her head in it.

Lillie had been asleep for only a few minutes when the nightmare came to her. The bloody mask of a twin's face, barely recognizable, stared at her in horror as she spat curses at the child in a voice reeking with hatred—a voice that could not be hers, but yet was. The last thing the woman in the dream did before Lillie's scream shattered her image was to raise her right fist to her mouth and laugh as she licked gore from the knuckles.

In spite of repeated heat treatments and a bottle of aspirin over the course of the next week, the pain persisted with an ever-increasing frequency and intensity. Any movement requiring even the slightest flexion of Lillie's right pectoral muscle made her wince. Had it not been for the arrival of a new child, Lillie would have attempted to endure the pain for another week before seeing a doctor.

Kay opened the front door and greeted Susan Kelly, who expertly cradled an infant in the crook

STEVEN W. WISE   [87]

of her left arm. The child squirmed contentedly as she blew tiny saliva bubbles at the corners of her mouth. Except for a delicate wisp of black hair at the crown of her head, the whiteness of the baby's skin was untainted. Dark brown eyes blinked against the brightness of the morning.

"Morning, Miss Kay. Look at what I've brought you this fine morning," Susan said as she stepped into the living room. "Her name is Heather, and she's six months old."

Kay sat down on the corner of the couch and extended her arms. "Let me hold her, Susan. If she isn't about the prettiest little thing . . ."

Susan looked up as Lillie entered the room, wiping her left hand on her apron while her right hand appeared to be pinned against her hip.

"Morning, Lillie."

"Morning, Susan. So this is little Miss . . . Helen, did you say on the phone?"

"Heather," Susan corrected.

Lillie moved to Kay and the baby and looked into the child's face. Susan glanced at the tall woman's face in anticipation of the broad smile that would soon light it, but the smile did not come.

"Crack dealers for parents, huh, little thing? It's a sorry life, isn't it?"

She reached down with her left hand, extending her fingers to their fullest, the great hand taking the shape of a bony claw, slowly encircling the baby's head. Susan watched curiously as the unusual caress was frozen for a moment before it took on a softer dimension, but she could not suppress the twinge of apprehension beginning to well up within her.

Lillie sat down wearily next to Kay and the baby, careful to protect her right side.

"Lillie, what's the matter with your arm?" Susan asked.

"Oh, it's a danged aggravation, that's all. Little Mister Dantley used his hard head for a battering ram and punched me in the side of the bosom a while back." She waved her hand as if to prevent further questions.

"How far back?" Susan persisted.

"Oh, I don't remember, Susan, a few days I suppose."

"It's been a lot long . . ." Kay interjected before being silenced by Lillie's icy stare.

"Kay, why don't you go settle that baby in her room?" Susan said. Kay got up and walked quickly to the stairs.

"Lillie Crow, for heaven's sake, why don't you let a doctor check you out? You may have torn a muscle or something in there."

"I might, if it keeps on. I'm not much on doctors—for Pete's sake, I don't even have one—and besides, I'm healthy as a plow horse, and you know it."

"You look like a three-legged plow horse to me, the way that arm's hanging there."

"I told you. The little tyke hit me really hard. Knotted up a little chunk of meat, he did. Anybody would need a few days of deep heat to get it worked out."

"Knot?" The word hung in the air. "Lillie, are you telling me that you've found a knot in your breast?" Susan struggled to keep the concern out of her voice.

"Yes, but it don't amount to a hill of beans. Can't be much bigger than a marble. I've had lumps all over me that . . ."

Susan's voice was steady and assertive now, and she looked directly into Lillie's eyes as she spoke. "Lillie, I'm going to call the hospital when I get back and get you an appointment. You must have it checked out. I'm not trying to frighten you, but . . . well, just humor me and do it, all right?"

"I don't see the need . . ." Lillie paused and looked at the younger woman who could no longer mask her anxiety. "You don't think it's *that*, do you? I told you, the child hit me as hard as I've been hit in a long time. That's what it is, Susan."

"I agree that it probably is, Lillie, but we're going to get it checked out. Please, just do it for a friend. Okay?"

Lillie raised her right arm a few inches as if to learn that the pain had somehow begun to show the beginnings of improvement, but she flinched from the effort and slowly exhaled in resignation.

"If it'll make you happy, Susan; but I tell you— the kid's head's as hard as a brickbat."

"I'll call back before noon," came the quick reply.

◆

MIDNIGHT

Lillie sat alone in the doctor's office and attempted to concentrate on the family photographs displayed prominently on the paneled wall to her left. The pictures showed a handsome family of five. In one the beaming parents were seated, flanked by two daughters, the son towering over them all. Lillie's eyes drifted to the wall behind the desk and the framed medical degree of Charles Elmer Needy, M.D.

"For a person who's not wild about doctors, you've had a double dose today, old woman," Lillie whispered to herself.

After a brief examination and discussion, the first doctor had quickly arranged an appointment with Dr. Needy. He had said little, other than that he felt Lillie should consult a specialist immediately, and that the lump was "suspicious." Needy had inserted a needle into the lump, drawing out material to be examined by the pathologist. His manner was firm but gentle, and he expertly side-stepped her questions, assuring her that there would be ample time for discussion after he had seen the pathologist's report. Lillie could hear his muffled voice on the other side of the door as he spoke with another man. The other voice, much lower than the doctor's —almost gravelly—answered his questions with uneven spurts of syllables. The pulse in her temples throbbed in cadence with the hammer strokes of her heart as Lillie Crow listened to the unintelligible pronouncement of her fate. The doorknob turned,

STEVEN W. WISE   [91]

the deep voice spoke once more, and the rustle of Needy's lab coat filled the office.

"Miss Crow, I . . ."

"Lillie, Doctor, please. I'm scared enough as it is."

Needy smiled thinly and nodded as he sat down. He drew a deep, even breath, and began to speak in a confident, almost upbeat, manner.

"Lillie, you and I have some serious work to do in order to help you with this problem. Dealing with these tumors, and . . . it is malignant, is my job, and I'm good at it when I'm given a chance. I'm a fighter, and I want you to be one, too."

He paused and forced her to meet his eyes. Her head shook slowly from side to side and dropped after a moment of bravery.

"How bad is it?"

"I'm going to be very frank with you. This tumor has been growing for many months—possibly years. We don't know at this point how fast it is growing, but it has very likely spread to the axillary lymph nodes, between your upper chest and armpit, and I can't rule out other areas. This kind of cancer has been known to invade bone and brain tissue as well. That's why it's imperative that we move quickly . . ."

She raised her head and her eyes sought his face —now a blurry image with a mouth that moved wordlessly in dream-like fashion. Her brain reeled as thoughts and images, both vivid and hazy, fought a sluggish battle for center stage. The great arms of George Crow extended toward her and then faded into nothingness. The gurgling cries of a tortured child filled her ears, the tiny face a mask of horror and confusion. Then the presence was with her, more powerful than the night in her bedroom, and she struggled to shape it into a form. Though drawn in to slits, she could discern eyes now, neither human nor animal, but incredibly intense with hatred. As they vanished, she could hear laughter.

"Miss Crow . . . Lillie . . . do you understand the urgency of what I just said?"

She blinked the man into focus and smiled crookedly before answering. "Yes . . . yes, I understand. . . . I'm a dead old bag, and there's nothing you or anyone else can do about it."

"Listen to me. I'll shoot straight with you—now and always. I would much rather have seen this tumor long ago as a tiny speck in a mammogram, but that's not the hand we've been dealt. It has done some damage, but I want to stop it from doing any more. I can't guarantee a remission, but I can guarantee that if we do nothing, this thing will continue to grow and cause great harm. This type tumor can have a tremendous growth rate. We must move *now*."

Needy was on the edge of his high-backed chair, his hands folded thoughtfully. Lillie had chosen them as her focal point, staring intently as they lightly tapped the desk with each emphasized word or syllable.

"I know how much of a shock this all must be, Lillie, but I cannot in good conscience waste a moment. You need surgery, and you need it now. Going in, we won't know precisely the extent to which . . ."

The intensity in her eyes as they rose to meet his rendered him mute. There was no fear or weakness that he could discern, only a steely resolve. She arose from her chair, stretching to her full height, and leaned slightly forward over the desk as she spoke.

"I'll be the one that decides when part of me gets hacked off . . . if it ever does."

"Well . . . yes . . . yes, of course. The decision is ultimately yours, but the urgency of the . . ."

Her eyes had not left Needy's and he was fighting the urge to avert his gaze as her long hand sliced through the air and silenced him for the last time. The stillness hung in the office as Lillie turned and walked to the door. Needy sprang from his chair and opened it for her.

"Please call me tomorrow after you've had some time. Please, Miss Crow."

There was no reply as she walked down the carpeted hallway.

When the doorbell rang at eight o'clock that evening, Lillie had little doubt about who was on the front porch.

"Come on in, Susan. I figured that was you," Lillie said as she smiled tiredly at the younger woman.

"We've about got the crew wrestled down for bed. Sit down for a minute. I'll be right back."

Susan sat on the edge of the sofa and mentally rehearsed the things she wanted to say and how she would say them. The friendly sounds of children's laughter and small bare feet romping on the carpet floated down from the upstairs rooms. After a few minutes, the sounds diminished, and then hushed completely. Lillie's house slippers padded softly over the living room floor, and Susan patted the sofa at her side in an invitation for Lillie to sit next to her. Lillie sat down and took the small hand in hers, squeezing it firmly. Tears began to form in Susan's eyes and she was helpless to stop them. She swiped angrily at them with the back of her free hand.

"Look at me, will you? This is exactly what I did *not* come here to do!"

"Child, child," Lillie said soothingly. "You know how much it means to an old woman to have someone who cares enough to cry? Don't feel bad about caring. I love you for it."

Lillie gathered the sobbing figure to her and they rocked as one for long moments before Susan broke the embrace and dug in her purse for a tissue.

"Lillie Crow, for heaven's sake, surely you're going to fight this thing. It's not like there's nothing they can do to help you. Think of these kids and this place that you built with so much of your life."

"Susan, I am thinking of the kids. I want to be with them as long as I can be worthwhile. But if I let them operate on me, I'll never get over it. Think about it. They're not talking about cutting a little hole in me and taking a few stitches. He's almost sure it's moved to other parts of me and . . . I'm too old to get over something like that. I've read things. I know. Young women take months, maybe years, to get to the point where they can be any good to anybody, much less a house full of youngsters . . ."

"Listen to you. You probably read an article in *McCalls* five years ago, and now you won't even talk to your doctor long enough for him to explain . . ."

"Honey, we both know the truth. If I go to sleep on that operating table, I'm going to wake up with almost half my upper body gone and the rest of it useless."

Susan started to speak, but Lillie silenced her with an upraised hand. "I've mulled this over all afternoon, and I'm telling you I'll be more good to everybody if I'm not cut on. It scares me more than the thought of dying, Susan. Can you understand that?"

Susan bowed her head and pinched the bridge of her nose before replying.

"Lillie, this is like a bad dream. I don't know what . . . Yes, yes I can understand that, I guess. But you're the strongest person I know, and I'd bet anything that you *would* recover and come back here. We'll find somebody to fill in while you're getting over it, and you can work your way back into the routine at your own speed. I just don't think that doing nothing is an option—for anybody's sake. Please, just go back and talk with Needy again. Just talk to him."

"He's already told me what he wants to do. And, now don't get me wrong, I'm not saying that he's giving me bad advice. I know he's good—a specialist and all that—but I just think I can fight it my way as long as he can his way."

"What way do you have, Lillie? I don't know what you think you . . ."

"Susan, the love of these little ones drives my total being—mind and body. I'm not so proud to think that I'm the only one who can love them dearly, but I'm a stubborn old fool. And the harder this thing works on me, the more I'm going to love and care for them. I'll bet you that I can do that for a long, long time."

They held each other's hands again in the silence and Susan studied the long hand engulfing hers.

"Lot of living on that paw, child. It's been bitten, cut, scratched, burned, mashed, fingernails have come and gone; it's been puked on, cried on, caught in doors . . ." Lillie tossed her head back and laughed easily at the memories. "They're not through yet, these hands." She winked at Susan and held both hands up, as if encircling a small object. "Who else you know can twist an apple in half?"

Susan looked up through her tears and smiled softly, shaking her head. "Nobody, Lillie. Nobody, but you."

"I won't go easy, child. I promise you that much."

They walked arm in arm from the living room onto the porch. The evening breeze whispered leaves in the maple trees around them, and the perfume from the pines at the edge of the driveway was a precious gift from the twilight. Susan tiptoed to kiss Lillie's cheek and descended the stairs to the concrete walk. She turned back to the porch.

"It's just not right, Lillie. It's just not fair."

"Me and you have dealt with a lot that isn't right or fair, Susan, and we'll keep on doing it because love is stronger than hate—strong enough to heal broken children. Maybe it's strong enough to help an old woman."

◆

Susan flipped the light switch in her kitchen as she walked through the back door of the apartment. She searched for a moment in her purse before pulling out a scrap of paper with two numbers written on it, and quickly punched seven digits on her telephone.

"Hello," answered a pleasant female voice.

"Yes, this is Susan Kelly. I spoke with Dr. Needy about a patient of his this afternoon. He said I could call him at home."

"Surely, just a minute please."

"This is Dr. Needy. How did it go, Miss Kelly?"

"Dr. Needy, . . . I don't think she will agree to surgery no matter what anyone says. She's strong-willed, and unless she decides to . . ."

"Miss Kelly, as I mentioned earlier, I don't discuss the condition of my patients with non-family members, but in this case, since you are a close friend and Miss Crow has no family, I'm going to be candid with you. Unless we remove as much cancerous tissue as possible, and combine that with courses of radiation and chemotherapy, the prognosis is extremely bleak. This kind of cancer often moves freely through the bloodstream, to the lymph nodes—where it almost assuredly already is, to the bones, to the brain. This is an extremely critical situation. If you are certain she will not agree to the surgery, please try to convince her to accept courses of radiation and chemotherapy. We might slow it down for a while, at least."

"I'll try, Doctor. I'll do what I can to convince her."

"Would she allow one of my patients who has been through surgery to speak with her? I know any number who could answer her questions from the patient's perspective. These are the 1990s. Techniques have changed greatly, even during the last few years."

"I really doubt it, Doctor. She's convinced herself that she would never return to the children if she's operated on. She thinks that she will have more time with them without the surgery than she would with it."

"Well, I don't know what else to tell you, Miss Kelly. As I told her, I'm a fighter, but I have to be given a chance to put the gloves on. Do what you

STEVEN W. WISE   [99]

can. Call the office or here again as soon as we can help."

"Thank you Dr. Needy. Good night."

◆

Lillie sat down wearily on the edge of her bed and looked at the wall calendar through the yellowish light filtering from the lamp shade. She smiled ruefully at the note in the day's box: *Dr's appt—9:45*. She reached for the ballpoint pen on the nightstand and scratched thick blue lines through the notation.

"Miss Lillie," came the soft voice from the doorway.

Lillie turned and motioned for Kay to join her. "Come in, honey. What's wrong?"

Kay sat on the bed beside Lillie and fidgeted with her nightgown, searching for the right words.

"It's all right, Kay. You know you can say anything you want to me."

"Miss Lillie . . . I couldn't help but hear Susan down there tonight . . . crying and all . . . and I know you ain't been feeling good, going to the doctor today and all . . ."

Lillie looked into Kay's eyes as they searched her face. There was no sense in trying to hide the truth from the girl. The trembling child of only a few weeks before was her friend now, her able helper. They had already been through more troubled waters together than most mothers and daughters encounter in a lifetime. The child who had lost the innocence of her youth in torment would have to bear yet another hard piece of life, but bear it she must. Lillie took Kay's hand in her own, and as gently as she knew how began to explain.

"The doctor told me that I have a . . . tumor . . . here, in my breast. I thought it was because the baby's head bumped me, you know . . . but the soreness wasn't from that at all. . . . It was this . . . tumor." She couldn't form the word on her lips—the ugly C word—the word of nightmares and dread. But the child knew of the word, and she knew that Susan's tears had not been shed lightly. She bit her trembling lip defiantly as she lowered her head into the lap of the woman who had returned her to life. Her teeth dug into the soft flesh of her lip. She would not weep and wail like a helpless infant, causing the woman to give even more of herself when she needed all her strength to fight. No, Kay had resolved it once and for all. She would stand with Lillie this time, not add to her burden. The girl waited until she was certain of her control, taking two even breaths and exhaling steadily, and then raised her head to face Lillie. She pointed to a spot behind her ear and spoke a single word.

"Smell."

Lillie's puzzled look gave way to a broad smile as Kay's invitation became clear to her. She bent her head forward and touched it to the side of Kay's head, and as she did, she breathed in the light fragrance of perfume.

STEVEN W. WISE   [101]

"It smells right on me now, Miss Lillie. Don't you think?"

"Oh, child, yes. Yes, it smells beautiful on you now."

6

CATHY HATFIELD maneuvered her car carefully through the late night traffic on Interstate 24, as the windshield wipers swiped patiently at the steady rain. The work shift had seemed unending, even though no unusual or especially difficult problems occurred. She had known since two o'clock that afternoon, and the desire to share the joy with the other nurses and aides on her wing had nearly driven her to distraction. But they would have to wait their turn in the proper order of things. She thought of Kevin, waiting half-awake at home, and laughed aloud at the image of the drowsy face that would soon be split with a toothy grin. They had been trying for two long years, and doubt and fear had begun to creep relentlessly toward them. The original plan had been to have a baby and postpone Cathy's entry into the workplace for a year, perhaps two, until just the right child care situation presented itself. Kevin's job was rock solid and his parents had helped the young couple financially to ensure a stress-free beginning to the marriage. But as the months drifted by, with no sign of a baby coming, reluctantly they had decided Cathy should begin her nursing career. Bravely they assured themselves that what would happen, would happen. Each hid secret fear from the other. But all doubt had been forever erased on this gray July day. Within minutes Kevin would share her joy and embrace her as a mother-to-be while the tiny embryo within her womb grew in beautiful form.

The traffic light blinked irritatingly yellow as the car neared the intersection, but there were no other vehicles within sight and she pressed the accelerator. Cathy Hatfield was three blocks from home— three blocks from sharing the wonderful news with the man she loved.

Kevin's long frame was stretched comfortably over the bed, a section of newspaper draped across his stomach. He smiled and blinked, owl-like, at Cathy as she came into the room. Without bothering to untie the laces, she pinched the heel of one shoe with the toe of the other and freed her foot, reversing the process with a stocking-covered foot. As Kevin watched with detached amusement, she removed her uniform and stockings, tossing them onto a loose pile at the foot of the bed without taking her eyes off her husband. She brushed the newspaper away with her hand as she slid into bed next to him, laying her head on his shoulder and wrapping an arm around his waist. He turned to face her and kissed the top of her head.

"My, my, Cathy girl, I'm waking up pretty fast."

"I meant for you to."

"You definitely got the job done, babe."

She took his hand and gently positioned it over the smooth skin of her lower abdomen, holding it there with a firm pressure. When she raised her head to meet his eyes, the first tears spilled onto her cheeks, and his face clouded at the sight of her emotion. Before he could speak she placed a finger over his lips and then quickly kissed him.

"Feel anything different down there, Kevin Hatfield?"

"What do you mean different?" He paused and pushed himself up on one elbow as the meaning of the question became clear to him. "Oh, Cat, do you mean . . . are you saying . . . ?"

"Yes, Kevin. Yes. I'm saying we did it. *We did it!*"

Their cries of joy were muffled as they embraced, child-like, and tossed about on the bed.

"Why didn't you say something sooner?" Kevin asked breathlessly. "I didn't even know anything was going on."

"I wanted to be positive. There was no use in both of us getting our hopes up again."

"I can't believe this," he said, returning his hand to her abdomen.

"Believe it, honey. This time there's a little Hatfield squirming around in there, and I want to cry and laugh and scream all at once."

STEVEN W. WISE   [105]

The rowdiness of their embrace gave way to tenderness, and they melted together as one in the dim
light of the lamp.

"All I ever wanted to do as a kid was drag a baby
doll around and play mother," she whispered.
"When I was only five or six years old, I'd cling to a
mother with a little baby 'til I was a pest, just hoping she would sit me in a chair and put that baby in
my lap for just a second or two. I can still remember
the first time. Momma always said I was born to be a
mother. Dear God, I hope she was right, Kevin."

"You'll be the finest mom that ever drew a breath,
Cat. There's no doubt of that, I promise."

"I'll call my parents tomorrow. You call yours
yourself, Kevin. News like this ought to come from
you."

She felt his head nod against hers.

"I'm glad Carl's coming over for supper tomorrow," Cathy said. "I can't wait to tell him."

"He'll love it, that's for sure," Kevin chuckled at
the thought. "He's a fine old fellow. There's more
to him than I thought at the start."

For several minutes they remained motionless and
silent, each lost in thoughts of impending parent-
hood, and each comfortable with the vision.

"I hope you don't feel like sleeping anytime soon,
Daddy," Cathy purred, breaking the stillness.

"Not a chance, *Mommy*. Not a chance."

◆

"What time did you tell Carl I'd pick him up?" Kevin raised his voice over the television noise.

"Will you turn that ballgame down? For heaven's sake, I can't understand a word you're saying," came the loud reply from the kitchen, and the roar of a crowd faded in the living room.

"I was asking what time you told Carl I'd get him."

"Why don't you go on now? It'll be four-thirty by the time you get over there. Start the fire before you go. Okay?"

"I guess I can manage that," he replied playfully. "Don't want any charcoal dust in the hamburger patties."

Kevin stepped through the sliding door onto the small concrete patio and soon had a fiery mound of briquettes in the bottom of the grill. He stopped at the kitchen sink to wash the stubborn black dust from his hands, then brushed a kiss against the back of Cathy's neck as he left.

Thirty minutes later, Cathy heard the front door open and walked into the living room to greet Carl who was maneuvering his crutches over the threshold.

"You're an absolute expert at that, Carl," Cathy teased only half in jest.

"I'd rather not need to be so good, child, but I reckon it beats crawling," he laughed as he made his way to the couch.

"I'm going to spread out the charcoal," Kevin said. "It's just plain grub, Carl. Hamburgers, potato

STEVEN W. WISE   [107]

salad, baked beans, and strawberry shortcake for dessert."

Carl solemnly nodded his head in reply as Kevin walked by and clapped his shoulder. "Great day, you two. I declare, if you don't quit feeding me like this so often, I'm going to have to get a stronger pair of crutches, and maybe a bigger pair of trousers."

He joined in their laughter as Kevin left the room. Cathy disappeared into the kitchen and returned with a tall glass of iced tea, a bowl of potato chips, and a container of dip.

"Work on this for a while, if you want. It won't take the hamburger king long out there. Everything else is ready."

"Whew, thanks," Carl said after two thirsty gulps of the tea. Cathy smiled mischievously as he gave her an inquiring look.

"We've got a surprise to share with you after supper, Carl. This is a big week for us, *real* big." She winked and quickly withdrew to the kitchen before he could swallow his mouthful of chips and speak.

The conversation around the supper table was light and congenial, with Carl content to ask an occasional question which would allow him to learn more about the couple who had befriended him. He was surprised at how quickly he'd grown close to them. It had been many years since a younger person had paid him any sincere attention, and he loved them for it. Kevin had been slightly withdrawn at first; perhaps he was wary of an injured old stranger, Carl surmised, one who might attach himself too greedily and not recognize when his welcome had worn out. But the reticence had been short-lived. Carl had taken great pains to ensure that he did not become a pest. He'd even turned down a couple of supper invitations for white-lie reasons, until he was certain that the desire for his company was shared by husband and wife alike.

"This is wonderful, kids, but I've simply got to quit while I can still breathe," Carl said, waving his napkin like a white flag of surrender.

"Let's move to the living room," Cathy offered. "You and Kevin both look like you need to stretch out a little. Drink a cup of coffee with me, Carl. You've surely got room for that. I haven't convinced this primitive individual of the joys of the stuff," she smiled coyly at Kevin, "yet."

"If it tasted as good as it smells, I'd have been hooked years ago," Kevin said.

"Ah, you . . ." Cathy said with a wave of her hand.

Carl worked his way to the couch and eased his weight onto the soft cushion with a loud sigh. Cathy placed a cup and saucer on the end table at his side.

"Seems I remember something about a surprise this evening," he said after he swallowed the first scalding sip.

"Why, yes sir, I think I do remember mentioning something like that," Cathy teased. She was seated on the carpet, leaning against Kevin's leg. She put

STEVEN W. WISE   [109]

her cup and saucer on the coffee table and reached up and took Kevin's hand, exchanging a soft smile for his wide grin.

"Besides our parents, you're the first to know, Carl, and we're both very glad it worked out this way." She paused for a moment and gathered her thoughts before continuing. "After months of worrying, and crying, and wanting, and waiting, we found out yesterday that we're going to be parents!"

Carl felt the lump in his throat grow with the realization that he, of all people—a broken down old man, just passing through their lives—had been honored with the glad announcement. He swallowed hard against the mass in his throat and looked first into Cathy's eyes and then Kevin's.

"Praise the good Lord, children," came the throaty voice, "I'll declare, this is a great day for an old man to have the likes of you two share a joy like that. Praise the good Lord."

Cathy stood and moved quickly to Carl, whose outstretched arms gathered her small figure in a warm embrace. She kissed him on the cheek and stepped aside so that Kevin could accept Carl's extended right hand.

"I knew you'd be happy with us," Cathy said. "With our parents so far away . . . and me not having living grandparents . . . well, I guess I'm making you an honorary grandparent . . . if you'll accept."

"With all my heart, Cathy. I never had a child,

much less a grandchild, of my own. I'm deeply honored. Thank you."

They embraced again and Carl fought against the burning sensation that felt like it would soon choke him. Cathy sensed his distress and avoided his eyes as she stood.

"I've about made myself bawl, for pity sake," she said in mock indignation. "This is supposed to be a happy night. I'm going to get the photo album, Kevin. What do you think? That'll perk us all up, right?"

"I'm not sure what this poor fellow has done to deserve that," Kevin said playfully, and joined Carl's chuckle.

"You're not fooling me, Kevin Hatfield. You like looking at pictures as much as I do. I think I'll bring you a cup of coffee, too!"

The next half hour passed swiftly as the plastic-covered pages of the big album revealed one happy memory after another—babies and beaming parents, backyards and scruffy little dogs, puckers and two-toothed grins, teen-agers decked out for prom night. With each photograph a spirited narrative tumbled from Cathy, giving way to Kevin only for the purpose of regaining her breath.

"For Pete's sake, Cathy, slow down," Kevin said. "Maybe Carl has a picture or two he'd show us. I'd like to know about his family, too."

"Carl, I'm sorry," she said, "I tend to get carried away about family things. . . . Forgive me."

"Don't be sorry. I could sit here all night and look

STEVEN W. WISE   [111]

and listen to you two. I haven't had a family feeling for a long time. This is food for an old man's soul."

"Come on," Cathy said. "We really would like to see some of your family. You must have one or two pictures in your wallet."

"Oh Lord, children, I don't carry much in my wallet in the way of pictures. Mostly I carry the pictures in my head."

He rolled onto one hip and fished the brown leather wallet from his pocket. It was shiny with age, and Cathy could see that the hinge was torn on both sides as he flipped it open. He turned through the photo holders for a moment and stopped suddenly as the eyes of his mother looked out at him from behind the cloudy plastic. She stood half a head shorter than the handsome man at her side, dominating the image and yet bonding gracefully with her husband. Carl removed the photo from its holder and handed it to Cathy. As Kevin looked over her shoulder, she studied the two faces, glancing up twice during the process to study Carl's face.

"You look like your mother so much! Wow," Cathy said, "look at that, Kevin."

"No doubt about it," Kevin murmured.

"That's what folks used to say, sure enough," Carl said softly. "That's the only picture I carry, I'm afraid. I had two brothers, both have passed on now, but I don't have any little pictures of them. Fact is, I cut that out of a bigger one so's I'd have one of them to carry with me," he said, pointing toward Cathy's hands. "Got two nephews in Oregon and a niece down in Mississippi, but we don't stay in touch very well."

"I'd like to see her smiling," Cathy said. "I bet it would be beautiful."

Carl laughed easily. "They didn't smile for pictures in those days, but I'll guarantee that she wanted to. Look at the corners of her mouth real close. Oh, yeah, she wanted to."

"I think so, too. You're right," Cathy said, peering intently at the woman's face.

"Everybody always looks so strong in those old pictures," Kevin said, "almost like they're trying to show everybody that they can stand up to anything."

"I suppose you're right, Kevin," Carl said. "I don't know about all of them, but those two were strong enough to stand most tests of this life." He paused and looked at the wall for a moment, lost in a thought that neither Cathy nor Kevin dared disturb. "I do know about those two."

Cathy handed the photo back to Carl who carefully replaced it in the wallet. She could see that his mood had changed—not dramatically, but as if he had suddenly become absorbed in thoughts on a different plane. She had seen senility force its way on the faces of older patients many times, but clearly that was not the case with Carl. He pursed his lips and then looked at her apologetically as he realized he had lost touch for a moment of unknown length.

"I'm . . . I'm sorry, kids. I went away for a bit."

STEVEN W. WISE   [113]

"Don't be sorry," Cathy said. "We made you take out the picture. I hope it didn't . . ."

"No, no, child, I was happy to share it with you both. No one's asked to see a picture of mine in years. It's just that . . . well, I got to thinking about . . . the woman I've got to find. She's not doing very well. I just know it. And I'm sitting here enjoying myself like there's nothing serious going on."

"You're doing great with that leg. It won't be much longer before you're good as new," Cathy said.

Carl shook his head solemnly. "I can't wait 'til the cast comes off. Fact is, I can't wait much longer at all." He smiled at the serious faces staring at him. "Kevin, if you'd carry these old bones to the boarding house, I'd better call it a night. And just let me say once more, this has been one of the happiest nights of my life. I'll always remember it."

Kevin helped Carl stand and the three of them moved slowly to the front door. Carl lifted his hand from the handle of the crutch and extended it to Cathy.

"There's a mighty lucky little baby inside you, child. God bless you both."

She watched from the doorway as the two men entered the car, and then disappeared into the night.

The cast came up too far on Carl's leg to allow him to kneel while he prayed. It had irritated him at first, to the point of interfering with his communion. But he had adjusted, and so had God, he figured. God had heard many prayers from many souls who did not kneel. He sat on the edge of his bed, the mending leg stretched rigidly to the floor, and hunched forward with his hands clasped in his lap. The words tumbled out in fervent whispers.

"Oh, my Lord and my God. Send me on to her. I know not how . . . but, please, send me on to her. You know her burden came to me tonight . . . clear and heavy. There's no doubt about what it was. . . . She's standing in the need. The Evil One draws near to her, and she knows You not. Send me on . . . come what may."

◆

The insistent clamor of the telephone filled Susan Kelly's small office. Without dropping the pen in her right hand or taking her eyes from the partially completed form on the desk, she lifted the receiver to her ear.

"Department of Social Services, Susan Kelly."

"Yes, please hold for Dr. Needy," came the clipped request.

"Miss Kelly?"

"Yes, Doctor, this is Susan."

"I'm calling because, quite frankly, I'm at a total loss as to how to get through to Miss Crow. *Days*," his voice drew out the word, "have passed, and this situation needs immediate attention. I realize that

STEVEN W. WISE

this facility is not world-renowned, nor am I, for that matter. I've contacted a colleague up at Duke University Medical Center—one of the most respected oncologists in the country—and he's agreed to see Miss Crow as soon as we can get her up there. That is, *if* we can get her up there. So you see . . ."

"Dr. Needy," Susan interrupted, "I can assure you that Lillie's confidence in you or the hospital has nothing to do with her decision about the surgery. She's just not going to agree to it—here, at Duke, or anywhere else."

Susan heard the heavy sigh on the line, like steam beginning to whistle from a kettle of boiling water.

"I'm just not used to dealing with patients, even older than she is, who appear to have no interest in prolonging life."

"It's not that. She just wants to do as well as she can for as long as she can with the house and the kids."

"That's what is so frustrating. With vigorous treatment, we can probably extend her useful life. Yes, she would be out of commission for a while, but . . . well, I can't force her. But surely she would accept radiation and chemotherapy treatments. That would be better than nothing at all."

"I'll talk to her about that again tonight. I'll do what I can. Thanks for your concern."

"Very well, Miss Kelly. You seem to be the adult who has the closest relationship with her, and you have the opportunity to observe her professionally

—in the children's home. Have you noticed any change in her behavior, or moods . . . even prior to the diagnosis, perhaps?"

Susan made no reply as the strange scene replayed in her mind—Lillie's long fingers encircling the baby's head, her features contorting into a mixture of anger and frustration, only to vanish in the next instant.

"Miss Kelly?"

"Oh, I'm sorry, Doctor. I . . . was just thinking about your question. In some ways . . . I suppose . . . Yes, even before the diagnosis, she was not herself."

"How so, if I may ask?"

Susan recounted the incident, and after re-living it for the second time in the space of a few minutes, could not suppress the nagging suspicion. "You don't think . . . her mind has been affected, do you?" she asked.

"As I said early on, brain metastasis is not uncommon with this malignancy. Please understand, I'm not being an alarmist. I'm simply attempting to gather all the facts I can, but it is very difficult when a patient is uncommunicative."

"Yes, I understand."

The silence on the line was uneasy as Susan waited for Dr. Needy to speak again. She did not want to hear what he would say, but knew she must.

"Miss Kelly," the doctor's voice was grave, "I would be remiss, possibly negligent, if I didn't offer

STEVEN W. WISE   [117]

an unsolicited opinion, given the situation with the children and all."

"Please, tell me what I need to know."

"I believe that you, or another responsible individual, should keep a close eye on Miss Crow . . . not only for her sake, but for that of the children, also."

The words thudded in Susan's ears, coldly factual, as if handed down by an uncaring higher power. She felt a twinge of anger well up within her until she remembered that it was just a man speaking, a man who really did care.

"Yes, doctor, I uh . . . We will do that, of course."

"Call the office at once if we can begin treatments. Goodbye, Miss Kelly."

"Goodbye, Doctor. And thank you."

It was after eight o'clock when Susan rang the doorbell at Crow House. Kay opened the door and Susan greeted her with a quick hug.

"Hello, Miss Kay, how you doing tonight?"

"Okay, Susan, I reckon."

"Where's Lillie?"

"Upstairs, getting her bath."

"That's okay, I just wanted to visit a while. Let's you and me talk for a little."

Kay plopped on the couch and drew a leg under her body while Susan sat down next to her.

"Whew! Tough day for me," Susan said. "How about you all?"

"Went pretty good, I reckon. Miss Lillie lets me help a lot nowadays." And she quickly added, "But I love it, all of it—the kids and cooking and all."

"I know you do, honey. You're a great help to her since she hurt herself."

Kay's gaze dropped to her lap and she began to chew thoughtfully on her lower lip.

"She told me," she whispered. "I know what she's got—the cancer."

Susan swallowed against the dryness in her throat as the cruel word hung in the air. The word should sound softer, Susan thought, less jagged, coming from the mouth of a child, but it was not so. The young woman and the child grieved at the sound of it.

"I didn't know if she'd told you, Kay. I knew she would, in time."

"I knew there was more wrong with her than a banged-up side, Susan. I've seen my share of hurt folks."

"Yes, I know you have, honey."

They sat in silence for a moment as Susan wrestled with the questions she must ask.

"Kay, Miss Lillie has been under a lot of strain lately, and I was wondering . . . well, if the kids are . . . bothering her more than usual, you know?"

The girl began to chew on her lip again and glanced over her shoulder up the staircase.

"Just between friends," Susan murmured, "to try

STEVEN W. WISE [119]

to help another friend, Kay. I promise, this is just between you and me."

"She's changed. No doubt of that," the small voice began, and then it quickly gained momentum until the words pushed one another from her mouth. "Like last night, when we put the twins to bed. You know, they're always full of it, wrestling and all, just being little boys. Well, Miss Lillie, she can always get them apart with a word or two, maybe just lift one off the other, real easy, you know. But . . . she . . . just took the top one by the hair—I mean a real handful—and jerked him off like a rag doll. Scared them both bad, me, too, to see her like that. Her face didn't look right either. I mean . . . it just wasn't Miss Lillie. Then, quick as it came, it passed. I could see she was sorry . . . but . . . it was already done. She's so strong . . . Oh, Susan, I don't know. I feel bad blabbing this all out. . . . I love her more than anybody in the world . . . but it scared me."

"It's all right, honey. Like I said, we're both trying to figure out how we can help her get better. I love her, too."

A door latch clicked open above them, and as they turned toward the sound, Lillie threw up a hand in greeting. "Hi, Susan. There's still coffee in the pot—probably stronger than black licorice by now—but you're welcome to a cup. I'll be down in a minute."

"No thanks, Lillie. Don't hurry," Susan called. She turned back to Kay and squeezed her hand and winked. "We'll figure something out. There's a real good doctor working with her, and I know he can help. Hang in there."

Kay managed a thin smile and nodded her head.

"Honey," Susan said. "There's one more thing. I need to know, right away, if Lillie doesn't act like herself, especially around the kids. Okay? You're not spying or squealing on anybody. Understand? It's a grown-up thing I'm asking you to do—for Lillie and the little ones. Remember that."

The girl nodded silently as Susan squeezed her hand a final time in reassurance. Kay uncoiled from the cushion and stood up.

"I'm going to my room," she said, pausing for a moment and glancing up the stairs. "Miss Lillie's got me reading books," she smiled, "getting ready for school and all. Me, reading in the summertime. Can you imagine? It's so I can't go to sleep now without reading some. It's neat."

"Yes, it is, Kay. It is neat. See you later."

Lillie padded softly down the stairs, tugging at the floppy belt of her terrycloth robe.

" 'Night, honey," she said as she passed Kay.

" 'Night, Miss Lillie."

The woman eased her long frame onto the couch and shifted her weight until she found a comfortable position. "Passed on the coffee, huh?"

Susan chuckled. "Yeah, it was an offer I could refuse."

"How're you doing?" Susan asked.

"Pretty good day today, Susan. Not bad."

STEVEN W. WISE   [121]

"Lillie, I won't beat around the bush. Dr. Needy called today and . . ."

"Susan, the answer's still no. I've made up my . . ."

Susan held up her hand defensively. "I know, Lillie, I know. I'm not trying to talk you into the surgery. I know your mind's made up on that. But there are other treatments that he thinks will help. Just hear me out for a minute. Okay?"

Lillie puffed her cheeks full of air and expelled it with a soft whoosh before nodding.

"You didn't really give him a chance to tell you about radiation or chemotherapy—things that don't have anything to do with an operation. If you would try them both together, he thinks you might get some shrinkage of the tumor—right away, maybe. I've checked. You don't even have to stay overnight in the hospital unless you want to."

"Want to!"

"I mean unless *you* feel the need to. They won't try to make you. What do you think?"

"I don't know, Susan. Seems to me that once they get you in there, they can do about whatever . . ."

"No. Absolutely not, Lillie. I swear. I've checked all this for you. The radiation is painless—just like an x-ray. The drugs do have some side effects—mostly they make you sick at your stomach, but that varies from person to person, and it goes away in a few days."

Neither spoke for a full minute, Susan having said all she dared and Lillie wrestling with her decision.

"I suppose I could try it—as long as they don't put me to sleep, and as long as I can go and come back quick."

"Oh, Lillie, that's great! I'll get someone to come and mind the house with Kay while you're gone. I'll drive you myself."

"No need of that, I can . . ."

"I want to, Lillie. Humor me, please. It'll make me feel like I'm doing something to help."

"Well, whatever."

Susan stood and clenched both fists in a defiant gesture. "Good, Lillie. This is good. I want you to fight back. Thank you. I'll call in the morning. They'll want to start right away."

She leaned over and gave Lillie a quick embrace and then a kiss on the forehead.

"We'll see what happens. 'Night, Susan."

The shadow cast on the wall was there when she opened her eyes from an uneasy sleep. She blinked against the hazy moonlight that washed the room. Soon the edges of the dark form grew sharper on the ashen wall. Lillie could see that it was more than a shadow, for shadows did not have yellow eyes. She gasped weakly, the saliva that had pooled under her tongue making a wet sucking noise. To her amazement, the rush of fear tingling through her body like electricity faded quickly, then vanished altogether, and she sensed a union with the form. It was unearthly and incredibly powerful. It glided forward—one step closer, and then another—until it

STEVEN W. WISE   [123]

stood at the foot of her bed. The head, too large for the body, tilted slowly to one side and the unblinking slits of yellow rotated with it and fixed on the woman. Its other features were unclear, but she could discern a mouth as it opened to form the word.

"Wreeetch." The word was drawn out pleasurably in a vile rasp. "Wretch, I can help you kill one. It will give you great satisfaction. Trust me, I have long known of such things."

Lillie was spellbound by the nearness of the form and the urgency of the scratchy voice. For a moment the thought that she would talk to it flickered through her brain, but she would have been unable to speak had she tried. The head tilted upright, and the form retreated to the wall as fluidly as it had come. Then it spoke a final word before it vanished.

"Remember."

Sleep, thick and dreamless, took her instantly. Five more hours of her life passed before dawn.

Lillie sat on the edge of the bed and clasped her hands in her lap to fight the trembling. She could remember the words it said, from the first to the last, and now her chin quivered with her hands as the first tear cut a tiny rivulet down the side of her nose. But beyond the horror of the words, two questions gnawed at the pit of her stomach, and she knew she had no answers. Why was there no fear of it, and why did she feel a union with it, a oneness with something so evil?

She stood up and swiped at her tears with the back of her hand. Her bare feet made no sound as she crept over the carpet toward the twins' room. Through the half-opened door she peered at the rumpled sheets. Jerry and Gary Imhoff lay snuggled back to back, their tousled heads nearly touching on one pillow. They were never separated, even in sleep, these two children who, before Crow House, had known few peaceful nights and had trusted only in each other. Lillie stood at the door for a full minute, looking, and loving, and praying to whatever god of goodness there might be—a god who could protect old women and children from the things of darkness.

◆

On the fifth day, the one which ended the first cycle of Lillie's treatment, Susan Kelly sat in the waiting room of the Out-Patient Clinic and flipped through the pages of a *Lady's Home Journal*, her mind unable to cling to anything more than splashes of color in the advertisements. Three emotions tugged at her without mercy—guilt, anger, and love—all tangled in a smothering mass in her brain. She despised the first two and clung to the last. She closed the magazine and tossed it onto the disorderly stack at her elbow. She looked at the door that would open any minute and disgorge Lillie Crow. She had made her decision, and although it was the right

STEVEN W. WISE   [125]

one, the guilt and anger would not allow her peace with it.

The call had come into the office at noon; the girl, Lisa, was four and still in the hospital. She would be released in two days to the Department. She would come to them with only three fingers on her right hand, her father having bitten off the other two rather neatly, near the hand. Punishment, accidently carried too far, he said. The child was bad about reaching toward the burners on the range. He was just trying to show her it was a dangerous thing to do. He had been unable to explain the teeth marks found in three other places on the small body. Neither could he explain the absence of the severed fingers, or even any blood, when he accompanied a sheriff's deputy to the house in an attempt to retrieve them for surgical re-attachment. The mother had been gone for six months. If a child ever needed Lillie Crow, it was this one, Susan thought to herself, but she knew it was unlikely they would ever meet.

She had consulted with her supervisor in Raleigh and had spent an anguished half hour with two board members of Crow House. But the burden of the decision rested on her, and she would have to bear it. Hasty arrangements had been made for the child, and Susan knew she'd been fortunate in locating a local family who would provide a good temporary home. Describing her second decision as such was nearly a misnomer; there was little judgement required. She would not tell Lillie about the child's placement.

The door made no sound as it swung open. A nurse steadied Lillie as she shuffled across the room. Susan had but ten steps to study her friend's face, but they provided more than enough time for her to see the strain etched into the eyes and the mouth that in recent days had seldom smiled.

"She's a little unsteady, Miss Kelly," the nurse said. "We think she should lie down here for a while, but . . . she insists on leaving now."

"It's all right," Susan said. "I'll get her home in good shape, I promise."

Susan took Lillie's arm and began to guide her toward the main door. When they had reached the edge of the parking lot, Lillie stopped, turned to face the hospital, and spoke the only words she would utter before she was home again at Crow House.

"Just saying good riddance, Susan. I won't be coming back standing up."

Susan opened her mouth to respond, but Lillie silenced her with a glance.

7

MABLE FOSTER was an inveterate reader of people. Through the years, many subjects had drifted through the fringes of her life at the boarding house, some for only a few days, others for many months. But no one had left without Mable forming an opinion about his or her character. Even the short-timers left clues scattered about like the clumps of mud from their shoes. An unwillingness to maintain eye contact, demands rather than requests, ignored thank yous for a kindness reaching far beyond the obligations of the meager rent, or, balancing the ledger, courtesy extended to her or another boarder, genuine smiles on beleaguered faces, truthfulness about cracking a pane of glass when it could have been hidden until after departure—there were a thousand ways to judge character. She had seen at least that many ways, she was certain. And she was certain that Carl Whittenburg was a man of character as well as religion. She watched as he paused and offered silent thanks at meals, and she listened to his quiet, well-timed comments when conversations drifted to the weightier matters of life.

She had clung to her church all her life and looked forward to Sundays as a balm to her soul, but she refrained from being the slightest bit pushy with invitations to her boarders to go to the services with her. She asked each one once, but never again if the invitee declined. Few accepted, but she never stopped asking. For Carl Whittenburg, she decided to break her rule. The way he declined her initial invitation made her decide to ask a second time. To be sure, there was courteousness the first time, but there was usually that from the least-inclined of them; no, Carl showed much more than that. There was unmistakable sorrow, nearly anguish, in his voice when he declined, and when she heard the sorrow she knew she would ask again.

Carl had been in his room for no more than a minute when he heard the soft knock on his door.

"Come in." He was seated in the chair near the bed and had his mending leg resting on the mattress.

"Carl, I'm sorry to bother you, but . . . I . . . Well, I just wanted to ask you something. To see if . . ."

"Come on in, Mable, glad for the company," Carl said, motioning for her to take a seat on the edge of the bed. She left the door well ajar and walked to the bed.

"I won't take but a minute. Got to clean the supper dishes and all." She paused for a moment to see if Carl intended to carry the small talk further, but he didn't. "Carl, a while back, first Sunday after you came, I asked if you might want to go to church with me. You said not, and it's been my rule as long as I've been here that I wouldn't hound nobody. But . . . I know you're no stranger to the Lord, and I was thinking that maybe I asked at a bad time or something . . ."

He smiled into her eyes and she felt relief with the knowledge that she had not pushed too hard or offended him.

"Mable, it's truly kind of you to ask me again, and I appreciate it—did when you asked the first time, too." He rolled his tongue against the inside of his cheek and sought the right words. "We're good enough friends now that I can talk straight with you about my reasons. Should have done it before for someone who cares like you do. I'm sorry I didn't.

"I grew up in a Pentecostal church—a small one, but a strong one. But one day, and it seems like it was all of a sudden, looking back on it, I looked around me in church and saw mostly old people. And then the preacher passed on, and a younger man came. But he didn't have much fire in him, and more old folks died, and no one new joined us, and then he went away . . . And then the church died. Reckon the truth is that us old ones scared the younger ones off, for, you see, we didn't try to hold the Spirit down when we felt Him near. The young folks went to the newer churches in town—the ones with pretty buildings and quiet, dignified services, preachers that shied away from the word *sin* and the like. You know what I mean, I reckon, don't you?"

Mable nodded solemnly, but said nothing.

"I tried, tried for a good while, I did, with some of the other churches . . . until the morning about ten years ago. A committee of deacons took me aside after the service and asked me not to come back unless I could 'restrain' myself more—that was the word they used, and I'll always see the man's mouth forming it. I was causing some of the other members to be uneasy—even the preacher himself sometimes, they said. I started to argue about binding up the Spirit, but I could see I was wasting my breath. I just walked away and never went back. I made my bedroom my sanctuary and my bed my altar, and I've worshiped my own way ever since."

He spoke the last sentence with a finality that nearly caused Mable to hold her tongue and leave quietly, but she was bound with him in spirit now and she spoke with a quiet strength.

"Can't say as I blame you, Carl, really can't. And I know you've got only what I tell you to go on, but hear me out, and then I'll leave. I guarantee you that if you go to the service with me tomorrow morning and you're moved by the Spirit in whatever way, you won't bother none of us, including the preacher. You hear something worth shouting about, brother, you shout. You get moved to tears,

STEVEN W. WISE   [131]

you weep freely and with no shame. The Spirit is welcome at our services. You would be, too."

She stood and moved to the door and when she looked back, he was still staring at the place where she had sat.

"Good night, Carl."

She did not see him at the breakfast table the next morning. With a growing discomfort she began to think that she had pried too deeply and opened an old wound that she had no right to open. She cleared the table and straightened the kitchen, all the while chastising herself for breaking her rule. As she arranged the damp dish towel on the oven door handle, she heard the muffled tap of crutches on the floor behind her. She drew a deep breath and turned to meet him.

"Morning, Mable," he boomed across the kitchen. "Got no proper church clothes really, and this slit pants leg flopping around don't look too fancy. But I hope it'll be all right."

"Oh, Carl, yes. Yes, you look fine as silk this morning to me." She began to fidget with the dish towel as the relief flooded through her. "Pull up a chair and I'll fix you a bowl of cereal. There's a nice sweet roll left, too."

"I'll get it," he said. "Getting pretty good with these confounded things. You go on and get ready. I'll be in the living room when you're ready to go."

Mable herded the old Plymouth through the light Sunday morning traffic, and in less than ten minutes, Carl could see the steeple rising above a row of stately oaks. It was not a large building, but it was well-maintained and hid its age adequately. Carl surmised that the siding had been either replaced or re-painted within the last three years, and the asphalt shingles covering the roof were in sound condition. Good signs, Carl thought to himself as he and Mable made their way to the front door.

"Nice building, Mable," Carl said. "It's nice to see a church building kept up like this."

"We work hard on it. Seems like there's always somebody who can do whatever it takes. Don't need to hire much contract labor."

She nodded toward the handsome brick-framed sign at the edge of the sidewalk and winked when she caught his eye. "Not a bad-looking sign either, huh?" The tall black lettering was hand painted in a sweeping style and read:

CHURCH OF THE SPIRIT

" 'Non-denominational' is the fancy word, I believe. Right, Carl?"

"Yes, that's the one," he chuckled in reply. "Another word might be 'mavericks,' I imagine. I like that."

Mable pumped hands and exchanged hugs with several members of the congregation, all-the-while working in introductions for Carl. The feel of sturdy handshakes jogged a dozen memories within him, and in a few minutes he was at ease with the crowd, bound with them, no longer a stranger. Mable directed him to a pew half-way down the aisle, carefully locating one which would allow him to stretch his plaster-covered leg for maximum comfort. Once seated, Carl studied the pulpit and the man sitting behind the modest lectern. Apparently there was no music director, for the man was alone. His eyes danced about the congregation, making contact with the worshipers as the first notes sounded from the piano. His eyes closed as his head began to bob in rhythm with the music. He was about fifty, Carl guessed, a robust man with square shoulders and tight skin under his chin. The mouth was wide and pleasant and fit well on the expansive face, which was the color of mahogany from the eyebrows down, in stark contrast to the whiteness of his brow.

"A farmer during the week, isn't he?" Carl whispered to Mable.

"Yes, he is. How'd you figure that?" she whispered back.

"No sun on his forehead, and years of it on the rest of his face."

"He ain't got much formal book learning, but he's got a head full of good sense. I can tell you that."

The piano stopped, and as the last note hung in the air, the man sprang from his chair, covering the five feet to the lectern in one giant stride. His chest expanded as he filled it with air, and Carl could feel goose flesh at the base of his neck as the preacher intoned the first words of the hymn:

MIDNIGHT

Res-cue the per-ish-ing,
Care for the dying,
Snatch them in pit-y from sin and the grave:
Weep o'er the err-ing one,
Lift up the fallen,
Tell them of Je-sus the might-y to save.

The power and splendor of the baritone voice reverberated in every crevice of the sanctuary, sending waves of energy to the listeners, and many raised arms of praise to the ceiling as the joy intermingled with the words of the hymn.

Tho they are slight-ing him, Still he is waiting . . .

"Yes, preacher, sing it out!"

Wait-ing the pen-i-tent child to re-ceive . . .

"Hallelujah!"

Plead with them ear-nest-ly,
Plead with them gent-ly . . .

"Praise Him, yes, Lord, yes!"

He will for-give if they on-ly be-lieve.

"Sing on, preacher!"

Carl scrambled to his good leg as the congregation rose as one in response to the preacher's motion for them to stand and join him in song. The

STEVEN W. WISE   [135]

last two verses were sung thunderously by the glad throng. But above it all, Carl could still hear the tall farmer, and he allowed the sound to carry him away to a dimension of praise he had given up for lost. When the hymn was finished, and while the congregation was still on its feet, the voice boomed over their heads.

"Where is this Jesus?"

"HERE!" came the united reply.

"How can it be?"

"THROUGH THE SPIRIT!"

"But you can't see Him."

"NEITHER CAN WE SEE THE MIGHTY WIND!"

"And you can't touch Him."

"BUT HE CAN TOUCH US!"

"Tell it, brothers and sisters, tell it true! Let's sing another one. 'My Jesus, I Love Thee.' Come on now, you know every word. Don't hold back. If you love Him, let Him know. He'll hear you."

They stayed on their feet and sang the three verses. Then they sang two more hymns, and the joy did not wane. When Carl finally settled back on the pew, sweat trickled warmly down his temples and he relished the feel of it, the honesty of it. He exchanged smiles with Mable who was dabbing at her roseate cheeks with a flowered handkerchief.

"Not too bad on the singing, is he?" her eyes teased him.

Carl made a small circle with his lips and shook

his head. "Not too bad. He any kin to Tennessee Ernie Ford?"

"Don't reckon so. Ernest Banks is his name."

The congregation settled in as the big man flipped through the pages of his Bible.

"Read with me, folks. Book of Mark, fifth chapter." The sound of the words seemed to fly directly at Carl, and it felt as if a big fist had bumped squarely against his chest. "Verse twenty-five is where we pick up the text."

Mable leaned toward Carl and extended her open Bible for him to share, and when he whispered to her, the words came out haltingly, "I . . . know . . . the words."

"And a certain woman, which had an issue of blood twelve years . . ." The strong voice faded and was replaced by that of a woman, rich and vibrant, with a melodious ring more suited to song than speech. Carl knew the voice, and he knew the face that soon came behind his closed eyelids. He had first heard her quote the verses when he was a child, perhaps eight years old, after she had returned from a long night with a gravely ill friend. The strain in her eyes did not mask the joy she radiated, and as the verses spilled from her, he first glimpsed the small frame of glass clutched in her hand. It did not seem so long ago now, here, in this sacred place. Again he was in the presence of the Spirit.

Ernest Banks' utterances gently pushed her away now, but Carl felt no remorse; this man was a worthy replacement. He spoke for thirty-five minutes on faith, and his fellow worshipers ebbed and flowed as one with him. Their cries of affirmation punctuating the place, their arms jutting skyward, they felt the pain and desperation of the dying woman turn to ecstasy when she touched His garment. The man paused, his dark eyes sweeping those of his flock.

"Oh, brethren, does it not comfort us to know that this power displayed two thousand years ago is just as strong today?"

"YES, PREACHER—TODAAAY!"

"She touched Him, in the midst of a near-mob, and He felt the power leave Him. How much of His might left Him that day? Is there any left for us today?"

"YES!"

"Brethren, I tell you true that the power that left Him was like one baby's tear compared to all the oceans of this world. Yes, Lord God, yes. There's much left to us. *If!* If we have the faith to take it. Broken bodies, broken minds, broken hearts—they can all be mended by that ocean of power, the great, rolling sea with no limits. May God forgive us when we allow a brother or sister to think for one minute that this was a tall tale told by some ancient fool and passed down through the centuries. God, forgive us!

"Like I know you must be from time to time, I am almost envious of those who walked the earth with the Christ. I often think I'd gladly trade my boots for sandals, the black bottomland I till for the sand and rocks of Palestine, the comfort of my dwelling for the rock crevices that The Baptist slept in if I could but glimpse Him one single time from afar, much less be close enough to touch Him. Ah, but that's the pitiful man in me, the weakness of my flesh that gives me leave of my senses, because when I wish for that, I forget . . . the One He left behind, the One He said could help us far more than even He . . . the Spirit . . . unfettered by time or place. He's *here* to answer the cry of faith of any who claim His name!"

"TELL IT PREACHER!"

"If the Spirit is not real, as the world tells us, then what is it that can fill up this room with such might? It's not the words of a country farmer, surely. It's Him!"

"GO ON, PREACHER, LET IT OUT NOW!"

"Do we work ourselves into a lather for naught? Do we feed on each other's emotion, like they say? Or do we simply give ourselves over, realizing that we amount to little, if we're not *bound to Him?*"

"*YES, OH, YES!*"

He lowered his head and gathered himself, passing a gnarled hand over his brow. When the preacher looked up, Carl felt the steady gaze fix him, and neither man averted his eyes.

"There are thousands like her today, beloved, with hurts and sorrows beyond the measure of man. I feel needs within this very room as surely as I know life in my veins. Don't let them wallow in the mire without Him, brothers and sisters. The Spirit heals, Jesus saves, just like two thousand years ago."

A single tear caught the light flooding through the windows as it oozed down his cheek.

"Seek them . . . and ye shall find them."

Carl heard little else during the close of the service. An invitation was given and a closing hymn sung, and then the preacher was milling with the congregation, but all-the-while, he steadily made his way to Carl's pew. Then he towered over Carl, extending his great hand over the varnished wood of the pew.

"Keep your seat, brother. I broke one once, too. Know what it's like." His handshake was firm, but not over-powering.

"Preacher, I'd like you to meet Carl Whittenburg, a friend of mine from the boarding house," Mable said.

"Ernest Banks. Pleasure's mine, Carl."

Mable threw up a hand to a friend three pews to her front, and dismissed herself.

"Brother Banks, I've been in some moving services in my time, though not lately, but none stronger than this one."

"Thank you kindly, sir, but I think you know that I had only a part in that. There's fifty people in this church could do the same thing . . . except, maybe for the singing." He smiled. "I do enjoy that more than most."

"Yes, preacher, you rightly should," Carl smiled back.

Neither spoke for a moment, and Carl sensed that neither could as their spirits touched.

"I . . . don't know . . . exactly what passed between us a while ago, brother. It's not important that I know, really. I know you won't be with us long, and that you have something to do that's urgent. Know this as you go. My prayers will go with you . . . wherever that is."

They shook hands again, and then he was swallowed by the crowd. As Carl maneuvered his way up the aisle toward the door, he could still hear the preacher's voice above the others.

Two of the other three boarders were sitting in the living room watching a pre-game television interview with an Atlanta Braves baseball player when Carl and Mable returned home. The other border flicked his way through sections of the thick morning newspaper, paying little attention to the television. He called out from the living room as he heard Carl and Mable in the kitchen, "I'll swear, Mrs. Foster, that chicken smell from in there's about to drive me wild."

"Won't be long, George. Just have to mash the potatoes and make the gravy and warm up the string beans," she called back. She had gotten up early and browned the chicken in a heavy iron skillet, then placed it in the oven to bake slowly while she was at church services. The meaty aroma had found every room of the house.

STEVEN W. WISE   [141]

Carl crutched his way toward the hallway, pausing at the kitchen door. He watched Mable pour milk into the drippings re-warming in the black skillet.

"Mable . . . I reckon I'll be moving on about Wednesday," he said. "I'll pay you through Friday though, like we agreed. It's been a mighty fine place to stay, I can tell you that."

She set the milk carton on the counter and turned to face him, a look of puzzlement on her face. "Why . . . sure, Carl. I . . . I kind of thought that you would let your leg heal before . . ."

"I have a checkup at the hospital Tuesday, and I'll go to that, but I know everything's all right . . . all right enough for me to travel." He smiled at her and raised the plastered leg a few inches off the floor. "I'll just stretch this thing out in the aisle on the bus. Won't be a big deal."

"Well, Carl Whittenburg, I'll hate to lose you, I sure enough will . . . but I know you're doing what you think's right."

They held each other's gaze until it was uncomfortable. Before she dropped her eyes, Carl nodded toward the stove. "Gravy burns pretty quick."

She drew her breath quickly through clenched teeth, making a hissing sound, and turned to the skillet.

♦

MIDNIGHT

Cathy got up from her chair in the waiting room and met Carl as he hobbled past the orderly holding the swinging door open for him.

"Well?" she chirped.

"X-ray's perfect, they say," Carl said.

"That's what we wanted to hear. I'll bring the car around. See you in a minute."

The ride to the boarding house was pleasant. They talked of the heat wave that had descended and the antics of the patients on Cathy's wing, and a half-dozen other light-hearted things. But it wasn't until she slowed the car in front of the house that Cathy realized Carl had been unusually quiet.

"Hard to get a word in edge-ways with me motor-mouthing, huh?" She jammed the gear selector up into park and switched off the engine.

"Cathy . . ." Carl's voice was hesitant. There was no easy way to say it. "I called and got a bus ticket for tomorrow. . . . I've got to get on down there . . ."

"Oh, Carl! You've done so well, don't get in a mad rush now. Whatever it is can wait until you heal properly."

"Honey, I'm well enough, and it can't wait. It just can't."

"What'll you do when you get there? Where will you stay? How will you get around?" The questions tumbled over one another.

"I've got some money held back. I'll find a decent motel. Lord knows, after being around you and

Mable Foster for so long, I could go without eating for a month and still be healthy." He tested a cautious smile, but Cathy ignored it.

"I really don't believe I'll be down there that long. . . . A few days at most . . ."

"How can you say that? Looking for one person in a whole town, and you don't even know her name . . ."

"There's more working here than just me, child. I'm the smallest part in this whole thing, there's no doubt of that, but I've got to do what I feel right about in my heart. Don't you see?"

Neither spoke for several moments, then Carl stole a glance out of the corner of his eye. She was staring straight ahead over the top of the steering wheel, thoughtfully chewing the inside of her cheek. The fingernails of her right hand pecked lightly on the side of the steering column. She drew a deep breath and exhaled through loose lips, and her features softened as she turned to him.

"Tell you what. Surely you'll let us have you over for supper tonight, to say goodbye. I'll call in a personal day. It's early and they won't have any trouble finding somebody to cover for me. I've done it for them."

"That's mighty kind of you, but there's no use in messing up your work . . ."

"It's no big deal, honest," she dismissed his argument with a wave of her hand. "It's settled then. Okay?" She continued without waiting for a reply.

"I'll pick you up around six, when the traffic thins out. Okay?"

"Great day, child, what can I say? I'd be happy to, but don't go to any troub . . ."

"It'll be more of the same old stuff, Carl. We'll throw something on the grill and open a couple of cans of beans. Does that sound like I'm going to play Betty Crocker to you? Come on now, I'll see you in."

Cathy was waiting for Kevin at the back door when he came home from work. His reaching hand never touched the knob as the door flew open. She grabbed his arm and pulled him inside.

"Kevin, how much vacation time do you have built up?"

He looked at her quizzically and raised his eyebrows in thought. "It's back up over ten days, I think. Why . . . ?"

"Sit down here a minute, we need to talk."

"About what? What are you so up in the air about?"

"Carl's gotten it in his head that he's going on down to North Carolina *tomorrow*, for pity sake! He's planning to wallow around on a bus for two days and then try to find a motel to crash in while he hunts for his mysterious woman. Can you just see it? Good grief!"

"Well, he's a grown . . ."

"Kevin, he's a crippled, old man! I know I've gotten too close to him, but I swear he's like a grandfather to me and . . ."

"So you want us to take him down there? That's it, isn't it? Huh?"

"Well, why couldn't we? I've looked in the atlas. If I can convince him to wait until Friday, we could leave after you get off work. We'd be all the way past Knoxville before midnight, or we could even keep on going. We neither one get sleepy on the road, you know that. And . . . well, we could get him settled in somewhere and be back here by Tuesday."

"I don't know. . . . I suppose the boss would let me have some time off. It is sort of an emergency, I guess, though I'm not exactly sure what the old guy's up to . . ."

"Let's just do it, Kevin. We'll both feel better, and besides, it'll be fun to be on the road again."

She took his face in both her hands and kissed him tenderly on the mouth. "You're as big an old softy as I am, Kevin Hatfield. You don't fool me for a minute."

"I've never been much good at fooling you about anything, Cat." They pecked each other's lips playfully as they parted.

"Oh yeah," she said, "Hurry and change, and go get him. I invited him over for supper." She smiled sweetly. "He doesn't know about this yet."

Kevin started to speak, but clamped his lips shut and left the room shaking his head.

Cathy was drying her hands with a dish towel as a little later she met Carl and Kevin in the living room.

"Surprise!" she announced. "No hamburger tonight. I found a package of chicken breasts in the freezer, and I zapped them in the microwave a little. By the time they're finished on the grill, they'll be finger-licking good."

"You mean you actually started a charcoal fire? With all that grimy black dust and such?" Kevin teased.

She rolled her eyes at him and stuck out her tongue. "Carl, sit down and take a load off. I've got fresh-brewed tea. I'll bring you a glass."

"Thank you kindly, Cathy."

"Me too?" Kevin called after her.

Soon she reappeared with two tall glasses, handing one to each man, and then plopped on the couch beside Kevin. She had planned to wait until after supper to make their offer to Carl, but looking at him and seeing the pathos hanging about him like a pall, she knew she couldn't wait.

"Carl, Kevin and I were thinking about you when he got home a while ago, and . . . well, we'd like to drive you to North Carolina. . . ."

"What? Oh, no, I won't hear of it," Carl said evenly. "It's a long way down there and I'm well enough to take the bus!"

Cathy held up her hand in a plea for silence. "Wait, Carl! Our reasons aren't all together noble. You see, we haven't been to the coast since we've been married. And after we drop you off . . . well, we were thinking how nice it would be to spend a night or two down there—maybe even go on down to Morehead City or somewhere. It would be sort of a mini-vacation. We were going in a month or so anyway, so . . ."

She could feel Kevin's eyes on her as she spun the white lie, but it was too soon to look at him or ask for a reassuring comment.

"If you could wait until Friday to leave, it would work out perfectly," she continued. "You can leave here tomorrow on a bus that'll stop at every wide place in the road, or you can leave with us Friday. We could drive straight on down there and it would all work out about the same. You might lose a day at the most. That about what you figure, Kevin?"

"Er . . . uh . . . yeah," Kevin stammered, "about a day's difference. Yeah."

"Hauling my carcass through Tennessee and North Carolina don't seem a fittin' way for you two to start a vacation," Carl said.

"Now, Carl, do you think that we've been having you over here and not really enjoying your company?" Cathy asked.

He furrowed his brow and passed a hand over the wild tuft of white hair, but did not reply.

"You'd have the whole back seat to sprawl out on, Carl," Kevin said, and Cathy smiled inwardly at his compliance with her innocent scheme. "But on the bus with that thing, you're liable to trip some old lady in the aisle and get sued." They all chuckled at the thought and Cathy knew the victory was won.

"You don't think there'd be much difference in the travel time, huh?" Carl asked.

"No, not much." Kevin said. "We'd both rather travel the interstates at night anyway, when it's cool and the traffic is light, and all. We're liable to drive straight through, once we get rolling."

"What do you say then?" Cathy asked. "Let's plan on it, all right?"

"Well, if you're sure it works in with your plans with no trouble. . . . I'd be grateful, to say the least."

"Hey, we were going to go down the same highways for almost the whole trip anyhow. It works out great," Kevin said.

"Well, that's settled. We'll work out the details tomorrow," Cathy said. "Come on, let's sit on the patio and sniff the smoke while the chicken cooks. The fire ought to be ready by now."

It was when he saw them standing at the grill, with the smoke curling around their heads, that the dread gouged at him for an instant, and then quickly faded. He could not affix it to anything in particular. It was obscure—blurred by the vibrancy of life about him—but it was real. Of that, the old man was certain.

8

THE TELEPHONE made a plastic clatter as Susan Kelly half-dropped it into its resting place. She reached up and methodically ran her forefinger around the rim of her right ear. Neither conversation had been especially long, but the tension level had caused her to press the instrument with too much force. The first call had been to Doctor Needy, and was the shorter of the two. He had resolved himself to the fact that Lillie was not his patient now, nor had she ever really been. He remained concerned and disappointed, he said, but Susan could sense the stoicism that runs like a strong thread in all physicians, especially those who deal with the critically ill on a daily basis. He could aid in the struggle of only those who were willing to struggle with him, only those who would meet the enemy face to face. Lillie was but one of many being swept along by the dark waters. There were many more; there would always be. Some he could help, if they would allow him to. Susan had asked painful questions and he had given painful answers. One cycle of treatment would have negligible effect on advanced cancer. Lillie would quickly become unable to cope with the demands of Crow House. Pain would soon become a great burden. Certainly, he would prescribe medication. It was a matter of months, possibly very few, at most several. He was very sorry.

The second conversation had been a conference call with the Crow House board chairman and three board members. She was the professional, and she had the closest view of the unfolding events. They had all agreed to that. Since she knew Lillie better than anyone, it was still her call. They would trust her judgement as to timing, but they were of one voice in insisting that contingency plans be made for placement of the remaining children.

She raised her head and stared at the acute angle formed by the long hands of the big wall clock, but they did not trouble her. It was the red needle of the second hand, relentless in its silent sweep, that taunted her. She muttered a curse under her breath at the carelessness with which it moved toward the moment of Lillie Crow's death.

It had taken several days for Lillie to regain a bit of the strength lost to the fatigue and nausea caused by the treatments. She was now able to eat enough to provide some energy, but it gave her no pleasure. It was merely a physical act she knew to be necessary. She spoke only to give instructions or to answer questions. When Kay attempted to draw her into light-hearted conversation, she could manage only a few words, sometimes a sentence, before the lines of her face froze, and the girl crept away. Lillie hated herself for it, but was powerless in her efforts to change. And yet she loved the children with a silent fury that clung tenaciously, like the last forlorn leaves defying the harsh breath of winter. But she could no longer give voice to her passion or touch what would identify the tenderness locked within her.

It was on the eighth day after her last treatment that the pain came to her bones. It began cunningly, more a promise than an immediate threat. She was able to cope with the faraway throb in her arms and shoulders and told herself this could be fought against. But within two more days, the faint throb had become a living thing, pulsating with each beat of her heart, and she could not escape its wrath. She passed the first night of torment writhing on sweat-soaked sheets and pacing the bedroom floor, hunched against the agony, pleading with the alarm clock for whatever mercy dawn might bring.

She lay curled on her bed, her legs drawn near her chest and her hands wrapped tightly around her knees, as the pale light oozed into the room. She had found an hour of unconsciousness, barely akin to sleep, and as her brain registered feeling, she braced herself in dread for what would surely come. She tested a half-breath and held it for a second before exhaling cautiously. It was still there, but to her thankful surprise, it had diminished. She forced herself to dress quickly before it returned full force. As she pulled on her clothing and sat on the edge of the bed, still the ache only taunted her. The light from the lamp beamed annoyingly on the cluttered top of the nightstand, and she grimly punched a number into the telephone.

The voice on the line was husky with sleep but not irritated. "Hello."

"Susan, I'm sorry to call you out of bed . . ."

"Lillie? Lillie, what's wrong?"

"The kids are all right. I . . . I just had a bad night. We need to talk, Susan, and I was wondering if you would come . . ."

"I'll be there in a half an hour."

"Wait! Could you maybe call that doctor and see if he could get me something stronger than aspirin? Maybe stop at that all night drugstore on Albamarle Road? I'll pay you back when you get here. . . ."

"Oh, Lillie! Yes, of course, I will. Be there as quick as I can. Lie back down now. Okay?"

"Now drive like you've got some sense, Susan. I'm better now than I was. There's no great hurry. You hear?"

"Yes, I hear. 'Bye."

She heard the click and hung up the phone noiselessly. She was thinking clearly now, thinking of the lives behind the other bedroom doors of Crow House, and the finality of it paralyzed her. They were no longer hers. No more could she shield

STEVEN W. WISE [153]

them from life's ugliness or teach them to forsake fear and embrace trust. The knowledge that she did not trust herself made her want to weep, but her eyes remained dry.

She could sense his nearness, and she remembered his last words to her. But now he told her not to weep.

With the muffled whump of the car door, Lillie started downstairs.

"Morning, girl," Lillie said as she swung open the front door.

"Hi, Lillie," Susan said, and gave her a quick hug in the doorway.

"I've put on the kettle. Come on in the kitchen."

Susan put a white sack on the table and pulled out a chair. She reached for the handle of the mug that Lillie offered to her, then withdrew a capsule container from the sack and began twisting the white lid. It spun with a series of irritating clicks.

"Those are supposed to be child-proof, honey, not adult-proof," Lillie said, reaching across the table and taking the container.

"Go ahead and take one. Okay? The directions are on there. They said you should eat a piece of toast or something. It's hard on your stomach, I imagine."

"I don't think it matters much whether or not I get an ulcer, do you?" The instant the words escaped her mouth, Lillie regretted the twinge of self-pity in her voice. "I'm sorry. . . . That's a pitiful thing to do to a friend like you. I'll never do it again. Forgive me."

"I imagine you've got a gripe or two coming, Lillie. Turn one loose anytime you want. It's okay."

"Thanks, dear, for the pills. Listen . . . the reason I wanted to talk. Well, it's mainly about the kids . . . and me. I'm not whining, but the pain I felt last night was more than I can tolerate and still do for them like I should. I mean, it took all my concentration to try and stay on top of it. All of it, Susan." She paused and moistened her lips with the tip of her tongue. "There was nothing left, Susan, and there ain't much left now. This has all happened a lot faster than I thought it would."

Susan scalded her emotion away with a sip of the steaming coffee before she trusted herself to speak. "There's no way I can sit here and tell you I know how you feel, because I don't. I just know two things. I love you and these kids, and I want what's best for you and for them both."

"You won't have any trouble with me. Don't worry. I'm running up the white flag. Don't you see? The fight's leaving me by the minute."

"I don't want you to stop fighting it, please, Lillie. I just want you to have some peace for a while so you can get some strength back. Just take one step at a time."

Lillie's hand slid slowly across the table and covered the tight knot of Susan's fingers. With the touch she told the younger woman that the shared knowledge of her doom should be cloaked no longer. "Oh, child, you are special to me. You know that, don't you? My, but we were a team, weren't we? Remember the first one you brought me—that little fellow with the broken ribs? We had him smiling and laughing in fifteen minutes. Had to stop because we were making his little ribs ache. I knew it then. We had something special, and so'd you, huh?"

Susan managed a nod, but could not look at Lillie.

"Cling to that now, Susan, and in the days to come. I will. It's the most comforting thing I can do —just thinking on all that. You think on it, too."

She squeezed Susan's fingers firmly, and then released them. "I'm going to leave tomorrow. I can get a room at . . ."

"No! No, you won't have to leave your home, Lillie. The board asked me . . . That's not exactly right. It was my decision, more mine . . . to make some plans, just in case you took a turn for the worse. I have temporary homes lined up for the children with good families here in town. All they need is a few hour's notice. It's all set."

"Susan, I don't mind leaving, really. It'd be less trouble for me to leave than them. They're all settled in and all . . ."

"No, I've thought this through already, Lillie. I've checked these families over with a fine-tooth comb. They're the cream of the crop. Trust me. I want you to be here, and that's the way it's going to be. The Health Department nurses will take good care of you, and I imagine you'll see my face around here some." She attempted a smile.

"I appreciate it, Susan. Everything."

"I'd better go clean up and get ready for work. You sure you'll be okay today?"

"I'll be okay. That Kay's turned into a regular whirlwind lately. Poor thing had to with me bumbling around like a sick plow horse."

"I'll make the arrangements with the families. It'll be sometime tomorrow afternoon, I suppose." It was almost a question. "Could work it all out by this afternoon without a lot of trouble."

"No, do it tomorrow. We're going to have a big day and evening in spite of it all. We'll read books and play games and pop up a tub full of corn. I want them to take a good memory away from here. They deserve that, at the least."

Kay was in the kitchen before the sound of Susan's car had faded into the asphalt of Morningside Road.

"Miss Lillie? Is everything all right?" The girl's voice sounded afraid.

Lillie stretched out her arms in invitation to the tousled figure. "Come here, Miss Kay. Sit yourself down on my lap. You're not too big just yet, you know?" Lillie stroked the hair from the child's forehead and kissed her cheek.

"We need to have a little talk, you and me—just woman to woman."

For reasons she did not question, the pain chose to lay low, reminding and warning, but not tormenting. Maybe it was the medication—it had made her queasy, and she knew that it was powerful —but she doubted it. After begrudging her the day, the pain would claim the night. But she willed the day to be glorious, and it was. Kay stood side by side with Lillie—preparing crispy, golden fried chicken, and mounds of mashed potatoes, and a deep-dish peach cobbler. Then they all sat on the floor and played games—silly, beautiful child games —and read books with dirty tattered pages. Eventually evening descended, and as the shadows took the light, they took Lillie's spirit and replaced it with misery.

By the time she helped Kay prepare the children for bed, she was spent in mind and body. Yet she knew that some reserve—however feeble—must come from somewhere to help her fight the night to come. At the bathroom sink she swallowed two of the capsules and half-staggered to her bed. She steeled her mind against the throbbing, determined to at least give herself a chance at sleep. But it did not come until he allowed it to come, and Lillie passed from consciousness with her fingertips clutching her right rib cage.

She awoke just after midnight to suffering that allowed her only the faintest attempts at drawing a breath. The sweat gathered in the corners of her eyes and added a puny dimension to her torment.

Without looking, she knew he was with her, and she willed herself to return the hatred that beamed at her like a filament of light, energized and precise in its aim, but she could not.

"Do not battle against me, wretch, for it is of no use." The words were clipped, barely above a whisper. "I can give you rest."

She rolled her head toward him, and as she did, the sweep of his hand passed over her body. With it came instant relief, and she greedily sucked air deep into her lungs. He allowed her a few moments to recover before he continued.

"We have a chore this night, you and I. Arise and follow me. The pain will not hinder you."

Lillie swung her legs over the side of the bed and sat upright, her eyes never losing contact with his. His body was of human form, and she watched as he glided noiselessly toward the door, his head ever turned to her. She was on steady legs now, descending the staircase, and she saw that the kitchen was their destination. The muted clink of metal against metal was the only sound in the kitchen as he slowly opened a counter drawer. He beckoned her with a motion of his hand.

"Choose a keen edge."

Lillie saw her hand and arm reach forward, as if disconnected from her body, and she could feel her fingers groping for a knife, finally closing around the coldness of the handle.

"Come now."

He retraced his steps back up the staircase and at

STEVEN W. WISE [159]

the top turned to the right, away from Lillie's bed-room. He paused for a moment at the half-opened door of Kay's bedroom, then resumed his pace only to pause again at the baby's door. But the last door was his destination, and he gently brushed it open. He stood beside the small forms of Jerry and Gary Imhoff, and though she could not see the features of his face, Lillie knew he smiled.

"I desire the blood of these two, wretch. It shall flow by your hand. Do not tarry."

She drew beside him at the bed, and her grip on the knife tightened. She could hear them breathing now, and her eyes had adjusted to the darkness so that she could discern the profile of their faces. In that instant, the seed of resistance took root in her brain. He knew.

"Do not tarrryyy!" he hissed. "Do them a great service. Hate put them here, and hate shall be with them all the days of their pitiful lives. There will always be someone to hate them, wretch. We both know this to be true. Do it now!"

Her arm began to ascend, and it reached shoulder level before the little girl's words came to her, and she was repeating them—love, love, love. The child's face filled her mind's eye and she could smell the fragrance of her silky hair as the breeze from the porch tossed it about.

He knew her thoughts. "No, you fool! It is hate that will prevail, always. Your victories are meaning-less. The world will take her back. I will take her back! Do it now!"

But the word was now a chant in her mind, and the woman clung tenaciously to it. Her grip on the knife diminished as the muscles and tendons of her forearm relaxed. Finally her hand trembled, and the knife thumped on the carpet and bounced under the edge of the bed. She ran crazily, veering down the hallway to her room, but he was behind her, relentless and taunting in his pursuit. She collapsed on her bed and raised her hands as if to shield her head from the vile nearness of him. The stench of his breath found her nostrils.

"You have failed me, and for this I will give you many more days of suffering." The voice was soft again—lilting in its mockery. "Before this night passes, you will fill your mouth with bed clothing to muffle your screams. And remember, this is only one night of many."

He laughed, finished with her for the present, but before he left the room, he savored the sound of her weeping.

◆

It was ten o'clock the next morning when Kay jerked her head toward the sound of the doorbell. The baby was vigorously stirring an imaginary batter with a long wooden spoon, the green plastic bowl locked protectively in his chubby legs. Kay stepped over him and through the kitchen doorway.

"Morning, Kay," Susan said.

"Hey, Susan, come on in."

STEVEN W. WISE   [161]

Susan entered the living room and glanced about in search of Lillie, but did not ask her whereabouts. "You all doing okay this morning?" she asked.

Kay did not speak, but her countenance gave Susan her answer. Susan stepped forward and wrapped an arm around Kay's shoulder.

"Where is she, honey?"

"Up there, in her room," was the hushed reply. "I'm getting really scared for her, Susan. It's like she turned into somebody else last night." The words were coming faster now, in spurts. "I mean, yesterday . . . we had a real good day, cooking and playing with the kids and all. And I know it tired her out some, but I figured she'd be better this morning. But . . . she ain't been out of her room yet. Just told me to feed the kids and leave her be. . . . And her voice and her face . . . I barely knew them . . ."

"The twins outside?" Susan asked. Kay nodded. "Well, you watch the baby for us, okay? I'll take care of Lillie."

The bedroom door stood open a few inches and Susan peeked into the room. Lillie was curled on her right side, facing the wall.

"Lillie?" Susan called softly. "Lillie, it's Susan. Can I come in?"

There was no reply. Maybe she's asleep, Susan thought. She coaxed the door half open and tiptoed to the foot of the bed. Lillie's eyes were open, seemingly fixed on some point in the wallpaper, but they did not turn to Susan when she moved to the side of the bed. The horror of the night just past was etched into the woman's face; the lines at the corners of her mouth and eyes were bloodless incisions and her eyes were devoid of even a glimmer of inner being. She had been reduced to the shadow of Lillie Crow, nothing more, and Susan's mind reeled with the impact of the specter before her. What could she say to Lillie? How would she say it? The moment of panic was fleeting as Susan realized that she could take all the time she wished. Lillie's eyes had not yet sought her and she stood three feet from Lillie's head. Susan kneeled in front of her friend and cradled the great pair of hands in her own, loving the worn texture of palms and fingers that had stroked a hundred children who'd been broken and sullied by other, wrongful hands.

"How can this be?" Susan moaned into the bed sheet. "What kind of god would let this happen?"

One of the hands stirred with life, and then two fingers reached over Susan's thumb and squeezed it weakly. Susan sought her eyes as they attempted to focus.

"Lillie, can you hear me?"

A nod, nearly undetectable, before the faraway voice. "It's Susan?"

"Yes, Lillie, it's me. It's morning."

"Who told you to come?"

"Nobody, Lillie. Nobody. I just dropped by to see how you all were coming with the children, to see if maybe I could help."

Her body shifted on the bed and she began to

uncoil from the tight comma that was molded into the mattress.

"Lillie, why didn't you call when it got so bad? I could have called Needy's office and brought the health nurse anytime . . . the middle of the night . . . whenever."

"It was . . . too late when . . . when it got real bad. I only had a couple hours 'til dawn."

"But it's the middle of the morning, Lillie. I just wished . . ."

"It doesn't matter now, Susan. I'm better in the day. . . . He doesn't bother me in the day."

"He?"

Lillie waved her hand as if she had misspoken, "It . . . I mean *it's* better in the daytime."

"Well, I'm calling Needy and getting you some stronger medicine today."

"It won't matter, but I appreciate the thought. Susan, where did you place Kay? In town?"

"Yes . . . well, practically. It's a little farm about ten miles out on Highway 11."

"I want to know more about it."

"Well, it's neat, very well-kept. Even got a couple of ponies for their kids. Three of them. Two older brothers and a girl a couple years younger than Kay. I promise she'll love . . ."

"The man. I want to know about the man, Susan."

"Lillie . . . I know I'm not as wise or keen-eyed as you are, but I've developed a pretty good feel for people the last few years. And as I live and breathe,

I just know he's a good man. You should see him around his daughter."

"Did they touch . . . when you saw them together . . . hold hands or kiss or hug, you know? Did he act like he was afraid to show affection . . . in front of somebody else?"

"Yes, Lillie. They touched beautifully. It was plain to see."

Susan thought she saw the beginning of a smile, but it did not grow. Lillie nodded her approval.

"I'm not getting up today, Susan. I'm in no shape for them to see me. I . . . I don't want them, especially Kay, to remember me like this. Tell her . . . that I promise I'll come say a proper goodbye when I get over this bad spell. Just tell her that for me. Make her understand, Susan. She is the most special one I've ever had. Ever. Tell her that, will you?"

"I promise."

"One more thing. Tell her I loved a man once—a good and true man, strong as a lion and gentle as a lamb. There's one like him that's a boy now. And one fine day when she's a woman and he's a man . . . Tell her not to be afraid to love him back. Tell her that."

"I will, Lillie, I promise."

"Go help her now. She's still a baby and I've dumped so much on her . . . It's pitiful. Go on."

"I'm going to get you some more medicine before I do . . ."

"Susan, I'm not that bad now, really. Honest. Just

take care of them and see them off right. That would be medicine for me now."

"All right, Lillie." Susan paused, not wanting to say it, but knowing that she should. "I'll . . . I'll check back on you when . . . uh, later."

"I'll know when they're gone, child. It's all right. I'll be okay."

The thought of Lillie in an empty house stabbed at Susan like a knife thrust. "I'll be back this evening and fix us some supper if you feel like eating. You won't have to worry about tonight, I'm staying over until you feel . . ."

"*No!*" The force of the word startled Susan into silence.

"No. I mean . . . thanks for the thought, but . . . I'll be okay. No need for you or anybody else to do that. No need at all. Just see to the kids. You can check on me later this evening, if you want, but you're going to sleep in your own bed, Susan."

"We'll talk later, Lillie. Try to get some rest now."

Susan watched from the doorway as the weary body slowly curled to face the wall, and within a few seconds, it was as if she had never moved or spoken.

The twins had few questions about the sudden relocation. Their entire lives had been lived in varying degrees of turmoil. This was the least of their concerns. They had been well cared for, and even loved, for the past months—things they had not come to expect from the strangeness of life—and

they were together. Above all else they were together.

By three o'clock, Susan and Kay had delivered
the other children to the foster homes and had
helped in settling them in. The busy drone of the
small car engine blended soothingly with the low
melody coming from the radio. Neither had spoken
since Susan had fulfilled her promises to Lillie, and
now, in the closeness of the front seat, neither
trusted their emotions. They were less than a mile
from Crow House when Kay broke the silence.

"I've got seventeen dollars."

Susan glanced at her, unable to disguise her puzzlement.

"Had it in my shoe when you all came for me.
Haven't wanted to buy nothing 'til now."

"What do you want to buy now, honey?"

"There's that big Revco up the next block. Will
you stop there a minute?"

"Sure, honey."

When they returned to the car, Kay clutched a
small, plastic sack in her right hand and cradled it
with her left.

"It's very nice, Kay. Something special," Susan
said.

"Thanks for helping me pick it out."

Susan looked in on Lillie while Kay packed her
things in the suitcase Lillie had given her shortly
after her arrival. It was old but sturdy, and not unat-
tractive, even by modern standards. They had
shopped several times, and Lillie had managed to

assemble a modest wardrobe for the child, and it was treasure, not cloth, that Kay carefully folded on her bed.

"She's sleeping," Susan said as she came into the room. "Breathing nice and easy, as far as I can tell. I called her doctor's office, and he's talked to the health nurse. She'll stop by later after we get you settled in at the Phillips' place."

Kay flipped the latches on the suitcase and looked quickly about the room, pausing at each wall as if to secure the images in her mind's eye. She turned to the dresser top and picked up the dainty, glass bottle and the scrap of paper bearing her best script. They left the bedroom and at the door to Lillie's bathroom, Kay put the suitcase down and pushed the door open. She rearranged several items on the vanity until the space of a square foot was bare. In the center of the small square, she placed a tiny bottle of Chanel No. 5 perfume so that the proud lettering faced her, and under the bottle, she slipped the note. It read: "I love the smell of it now. Love, Kay."

They walked to the car arm in arm, and as Kay took her seat beside Susan, her chin trembled but the girl did not cry. She allowed herself a final look at the big house. And the stillness of the place, and the stillness of the solitary woman inside was haunting.

◆

MIDNIGHT

In a place not of the earth, yet very near it, two voices rose above the discordant babble filling the heavy shadows. The greater of the two growled and threatened, while the other muttered fawningly in a feeble attempt at self-defense. Other voices, raspy and cruel, hurled curses at the failed one.

"Silence!" commanded the tall form that towered over the legion. His yellow eyes burned with wrath as they swept first over the throng about him and then the deserted figure kneeling at his feet.

"It is a matter that even *your* feeble intellect should be able to grasp, heathen. You have failed me miserably." The silence was ominous as he allowed the words to hang in the air. "And yet, for reasons unclear to me, I feel that you have potential. The level of your hatred for them is excellent. Much greater than some who even now curse you in your failure." His eyes darted about and many heads quickly dropped in deference to the indictment.

"Thus, you will seek out the old fool yet again. His crippling gave me little pleasure, and he continues to be a distraction."

The great head inched forward until it hovered over the smaller head. "I do not wish to ever see this distraction within a hundred miles of the wretch who succors the child-humans. It would greatly interfere with my pleasure, and this would displease me no end. Do you understand me?"

Although still bowed, the small head nodded vigorously.

"Then off with the lot of you! Do you not each

STEVEN W. WISE   [169]

have tasks?" And with a violent wave of his arm, the horde departed in great haste.

He stood alone now and allowed himself a moment of reflection upon each of his agents, secure in the knowledge that all would do all within their power to carry out his desires. The crooked smile spread across his countenance and sharpened his features as he thought of his self-appointed task for the night. Then he vanished into the gloom.

9

CARL SAT alone on Mable Foster's front porch, his crutches leaning against the peeling white paint of the frame post. He let his eyes wander without purpose up and down the quiet street and decided that his initial impression had been very accurate—save for more two-story houses, it was a street much like his own. The houses were modest, yet had a character that only the passing of forty or fifty seasons can bestow, and the trees, too, had withstood the test of time and had woven deep roots into the small yards and under the cracked sidewalks. He thought about the place he was seeking, the home of the woman in peril. Was it even a house? Perhaps it was a mobile home, a retirement home, a hospital? His reverie was broken by the slap of the screen door behind him.

"Thought you and your young friends might like something to snack on in the car," Mable said, setting a plastic-topped coffee can next to Carl's suitcase. "Chocolate chip, just baked them this after-noon. And if you tell me you've had better, you're fibbing."

"Thank you, Mable, that's mighty nice of you. I think I'd better let the kids eat most of them," he said, shaking his head and patting his stomach.

Mable moved a metal chair even with his and sat down. "How long before they come, you think?"

"Anytime now. Cathy'll have the car loaded and ready for Kevin when he gets home from work. Says they'll 'hit the road running'."

Mable nodded and returned Carl's smile. "Been a real pleasure having you stay in my house, Carl. Had crippled folks before, but none that didn't act like it. You take care of yourself, you hear?"

"You do the same, Mable. The pleasure's been mine. I wish I'd had the chance to know you better, and your church, too."

"No law says you can't come back sometime, you know."

"Never know, that's the truth," he said, and though they both knew he never would, the words felt good.

The light blue Chevrolet four-door braked to a stop at the curb, the trunk lid popping free of its latch even before anyone emerged. Carl reached for his crutches and rocked forward on his good leg. Kevin's long legs carried him quickly up the side-walk and propelled him onto the porch.

"Hey, Mrs. Foster, how're you this evening?" he

asked. Then, without waiting for an answer, he reached for the suitcase. "This it, Carl?"

"That'll do it, Kevin. You'll like what's in the can."

" 'Bye, Mrs. Foster."

"Goodbye to you, Kevin," she said and waved to Cathy as her upper body emerged from the trunk.

Carl negotiated the three steps down to the walk and then paused. "Say goodbye to the preacher for me, will you, Mable? He'll be with me for a long time."

"I will," she replied, and waved a final time.

Cathy opened the rear door for Carl as he approached the car. "Hey there, Carl. Ready to ride?"

"Raring to go, girl."

"Got you a couple of pillows so you can prop up against the other door. You can stretch your leg out on the seat. I think you'll be pretty comfortable. I know it'll be better than riding a bus," she teased.

"Can't argue with that," he said as he handed her the crutches.

"Anybody that's got to go to the bathroom's in trouble," Kevin said. "Next stop's Nashville."

"Oh, Kevin, for Pete's sake, just drive, will you," Cathy said, landing a playful punch on his shoulder. "Don't pay any attention to him, Carl. He turns into some kind of robot when he gets on the interstate—thinks it's against the law to stop 'til he gets the whole leg done."

"Interstates are for driving, not stopping," Kevin

egged her on. "Can't make time if the wheels aren't rolling."

"Just listen to you, Mr. Road Warrior of Kentucky!" she huffed. Satisfied, Kevin laughed at her scowl and threw up his right hand to ward off her next jab.

"What kind of music do you like?" he asked, looking at Carl. "We have mostly country, some rockabilly, a little hard rock . . . you name it."

"Only one I recognize is country, Kevin, but it doesn't matter to me."

"Country it is, then. Pull out George and Tammy, Cat, and let's put some miles behind us."

By eight forty-five, Interstate 24 had merged with Interstate 65 and the traffic thickened as they entered the metropolitan area of Nashville, Tennessee. Several miles south of the highway, the downtown skyline jutted into the twilight with a big-city arrogance that only the most jaded residents could ignore.

"Isn't it beautiful?" Cathy added. "Wish we could see it in the dark, all lit up."

"Be good and dark by Knoxville," Kevin said. "You'll get an eyeful of lights there. Only a hundred and seventy-five miles . . . I figure we'll be there about eleven thirty or so . . ."

"You'd better be including at least a twenty minute stop soon, mister . . ." Cathy began.

"All right, all right. I need to gas up anyway. At the next burger joint exit, we'll grab a sandwich and chomp on those chocolate chip cookies back there. Huh, Carl?"

"I could go for that, all right," Carl answered.

Within thirty minutes, they had picked up Interstate 40, passed by the downtown business area, and crossed the river with the steady stream of vehicles roaring east into the dusk. After twenty miles, the traffic thinned nicely, and Kevin set the cruise control on seventy miles an hour. The conversation was animated as the mile markers flashed by in the headlights. Without warning Carl became aware of a twinge of uneasiness—unidentifiable, yet genuine— but he said nothing, and it soon passed.

◆

Fifteen miles beyond the eastern city limits of Knoxville, the dark blue paint of a van at the side of the convenience store building blended evenly with the murkiness. The blocky vehicle was parked just beyond the white glare cast by the storefront and gasoline canopy lights. The only light from the front seat was projected by the pair of tiny orange dots that flashed every few seconds just above the dashboard; then tight trails of smoke would jet from the open windows to be whisked away by the night wind. The occupants had sat in silence for seven cigarettes each, and when the man on the passenger side spoke, his voice was coated with the smoke.

"It's almost midnight, Virgil."

"I know what time it is," the other man sneered.

"Well, it's just that we've been sitting here for an hour and a half and ain't seen nobody worth doing. I say we move on."

"The storekeep ain't seen us. No reason to get in a hurry. We'll try another half hour. This place . . . just feels right. Just keep your britches on."

The other man muttered more to himself than to the driver. He crumpled the empty cigarette pack in his right hand and reached down between the seats with his left, fumbling for the carton. His fingertips brushed against the cool steel tubes of the double-barrelled shotgun, and he allowed his fingers to traverse the length of the sinister weapon. It was less than two cigarette cartons long, he judged. He found the twin hammers and smiled to himself at the response they always commanded when they snicked back to look like fangs in the open mouth of a rattlesnake. He fondled the barrels of the gun until he found the gaping, ten-gauge holes in which he could easily fit his meaty thumb.

The headlights of a car swerved into the driveway, followed by a Chevrolet sedan that eased to a stop at the first set of gasoline pumps.

"Ohhh, myyyy. Catch the chickie riding shotgun!" the man on the passenger side hooted excitedly.

"Shut up, you ninny!" the driver hissed. The woman got out of the car and stood by the open door, speaking to someone in the backseat. She placed her hands on her hips and as she arched her back luxuriously against her taunt muscles, her figure was profiled in the light.

"Virgil! Just lookie there. Out-of-state plates, too. Just her and her old man."

"Simmer down, Bud. There's somebody in the backseat, too." The voice was calm and calculating, and the man's head did not move.

The woman opened the back door, reached inside, and retrieved a pair of crutches. Slowly, a plaster-covered leg emerged from the doorway, and a man took the girl's arm and gained his feet.

"It's an old cripple, Virgil!" The man could scarcely suppress his excitement. "Couldn't be no better!"

The driver continued to watch in silence for a moment, and the other man dared say no more. When the driver finally spoke, it was with the same detachment as before.

"Get me the ice pick."

The glove box door flopped open and the rustle of objects both soft and metallic filled the close space of the van. The driver's eyes did not move from the car, and when the rustling stopped, he held out an upturned palm, like an operating surgeon demanding an instrument. His fingers closed comfortably around the wooden handle as his left hand found the door latch. He spoke as if coaxing a child to obey his instructions.

"That's right, pretty boy. . . . Set the nozzle just right. . . . Come on now. Set the lock and let her pump. . . . No need for you to hang around."

STEVEN W. WISE   [177]

The car's driver took one last glance at the digits flicking past on the pump display and, satisfied, began to stride toward the building. The door latch clicked softly and the van driver slid from behind the wheel, quietly returning the door to the body of the vehicle, but not latching it. He walked casually to the edge of the light and stole a glance through the plate glass front of the store. With the quickness of an animal, he darted to the right rear tire of the car and made one calculated thrust with the ice pick. Then he was part of the shadows again. He had been in the light for exactly three seconds. He slithered behind the steering wheel and pulled the door behind him, still careful not to slam it, and fixed his gaze on the blue car.

"Gooood, Virgil. Pretty work," the other man whispered, taking the ice pick and returning it to the glove box.

Kevin walked to the gas pump and topped off the tank before returning to the store. After he paid the bill, all three travelers approached the car. Within moments Kevin had assisted Carl to his backseat position, and had taken the passenger side of the front seat. The engine whined to life and the car passed from the light of the canopy. Only two people heard the door of the van shut tightly.

"Everybody all right?" Kevin asked.

"Fresh as a daisy," Cathy chirped. "The chocolate in those cookies wired me up. I couldn't get sleepy if I tried."

"Not to mention the giant Snicker's bar," Kevin said.

"Hey, I was just trying to leave more of the cookies for you and Carl," she replied.

"Don't leave anymore for me," Carl said, "I'm done for the night."

"Why don't you get a couple hours' sleep, Carl?" Kevin said. "I figure about that much will get us through the mountains and into North Carolina. We'll stop again in Asheville and take stock."

The smooth voice of Randy Travis filled the car as Cathy wedged comfortably into the driver's seat and set the cruise control. The highway was hers, she thought to herself, and she began to mouth the lyrics of the song along with the country star. She glanced into the rear-view mirror and saw only one set of headlights; it was a quarter of a mile behind.

"How long you figure, Virgil?"

"Somewhere in the mountains, Bud. Somewhere in those pretty hills of Tennessee." Both men cackled with delight.

Cathy first noticed the drag on the right side of the car as she negotiated a tight curve to the left, but she attributed it to the sharpness of the mountain curve. She drove another mile before she decided otherwise.

"Kevin, something's pulling on the right side of the car."

"What do you mean, 'pulling'?" he asked.

STEVEN W. WISE   [179]

"Can't you feel it? Just . . . pulling, I don't know."

"Pull over and let me check it out," he instructed.

Cathy braked steadily and pulled onto the paved shoulder of the highway, the headlight beam glancing off the low steel guardrail. Neither she nor Kevin noticed the pair of headlights that blinked off three hundred yards behind them. Kevin fished under the front seat for a moment and retrieved a flashlight before leaving the car. Cathy hurried to the right side of the car and found him staring down the flashlight beam at the offending tire.

"Looks like a slow leak. Bet it doesn't have more than eight or ten pounds of air left in it. I'll have to change it."

"I can't believe this," Cathy said dejectedly.

"At least it's almost level here," he said. "We're lucky for that, I suppose. Tell Carl what's happened. No need of him getting up. Open the glove box and pop the trunk, will you?"

When he turned toward the trunk, the headlights of the van were a hundred yards away and closing fast. He watched the big vehicle lumber to a stop within twenty feet of him. Cathy's head popped out of the car and she shot a glance at Kevin.

"Good Samaritans, I guess," he said. "Maybe they'll leave the headlights on us while I fix it."

Both doors of the van opened at once and two figures appeared, remaining behind the beams of light as Kevin strained to see. The person on the driver's side was slight of build and wore a cap, while the passenger was nearly a head taller and much heavier. The smaller man spoke first.

"Trouble, folks?" drawled the gravelly voice.

"Not much, just a flat," Kevin replied, trying to ignore the apprehension mounting inside him.

"Well, Bud, you reckon we could be of assistance to these folks?"

The big man answered with an unintelligible grunt and passed his left hand over his head.

"Ain't much for talking around strangers, Bud ain't," the little man said, and sauntered forward until he stood at the rear bumper of the car. The stale-smoke smell of him drifted to Cathy's nostrils. Thin clouds covered the half-moon, but she could see the crooked smile on his face.

"Don't be bashful now, Bud. Come on up here and lend a strong arm to these folks."

"I can change the tire myself," Kevin said, "if you'd just let me use your headlights . . ."

"Nah, pardner." The voice had lost its friendliness. "We got something else in mind." The little man took a quick step back as the big man drew even with him. "Show him, Bud."

The big man's right forearm extended from behind him and the sound of two gun hammers cocking could be heard distinctly in the stillness. Kevin sucked in his breath an instant before Cathy saw the weapon.

"Oh!" The cry escaped her feebly, but it was still pleasing to the man with the shotgun.

STEVEN W. WISE   [181]

"Easy now, easy," the little man said soothingly. "No time to get jumpy. Bud spooks easy, he does."

Carl had pulled himself from the backseat and stood on his good leg, leaning against the car. He was speechless with horror as his eyes took in the unreal scene before him. His right hand slowly reached out for Cathy's arm, but the little man snarled and pointed at him.

"Don't touch her, Gramps! Not if you want to live to die in bed. If he moves his arm again, Bud, show him what buckshot does to plaster."

The big man laughed stupidly as the other continued to speak.

"Here's the deal. Car comes by . . . and I hear one coming now . . . everybody stand easy and look natural. . . . It won't stop nohow. Can't help you none. Just listen to me."

The diesel engine of a tractor-trailer rig droned closer, and Kevin considered the odds. His tongue passed nervously over his lips and he wiped sweat from his palms on his jeans.

"I know what you're thinking, pardner, and it ain't very smart," the little man warned. "He *will* shoot the old man's leg off. Now turn around and lean in the trunk like you was fishing for the jack, and stay in there!"

The big rig slowed noticeably, but showed no sign of stopping. Then it roared into the night.

"That was good, buddy . . . real smart. I hope you can keep your cool a little longer. This here's the deal. We're going to borrow the little woman for a while." Kevin took a quick step at him only to feel the barrels of the shotgun jab into his ribs. "Use your head, hero. We ain't gonna do nothing to her that you ain't done a hundred times. You can pick her up at the next exit down the line, safe and sound, no worse for the wear. . . . Can't use one up, ya' know."

"You filthy . . ."

"I'm getting tired of you, hero!"

Carl hopped a step forward and looked into the face of the little man. "In the name of God, man, stop this . . ." An open hand flashed out and popped loudly against Carl's cheek. The only sound was Cathy's soft weeping.

"Time to stop talking and get on with it, Bud. Cover the hero." He moved toward Cathy and tightly clamped his hand around her arm. A guttural sound rose up in Kevin's throat.

"Kevin!" she screamed. "Don't let them kill you!"

The little man was the first to see the stranger approaching in the distance, beyond Cathy's shoulder, and he froze.

"What the . . ."

The stranger walked unhurriedly, although his great strides devoured the paved shoulder of the highway. A mane of white hair billowed with the breeze, and a white shirt glowed in the faint moonlight. One by one, all heads turned and watched his approach. He did not stop until he stood a yard from the little man, whose neck formed an unnatural angle with his body as he stared into the long face. Bud's mouth hung open and groped for words that would not come, and he moved the muzzle of the shotgun from Kevin to the stranger.

He spoke the words softly, but they were a command. "Release the woman."

Cathy felt the little man's grip loosen and she jerked her arm free. The little man retreated cautiously toward his partner and silently wrenched the shotgun from Bud's hands and trained it on the tall man clad in denim coveralls. "Listen, farmer, I don't know where in . . ."

"Silence!" In a blur of motion the stranger took one step toward the gun and before the little man could pull the triggers, he wedged his thumb in front of the hammers and yanked the weapon free. He carried it in his left hand as he walked to the passenger door of the van. He placed his right hand at the bottom of the window opening, and with no apparent effort, in one motion ripped the door from its hinges and flung it over the guardrail as the eerie groan of rending metal echoed in the valley below. He reached across the front seat, removed the ignition key, and threw it into the valley.

"Sweet Jesus, Thou hast delivered us!" Carl whispered to himself as he witnessed the spectacle.

"Come." The command was directed to the owners of the van, who hesitated and then shuffled forward compliantly.

"L-l-listen, mister . . ."

"Be silent in your last moments. Seat yourselves

and do not move." He pointed to the front seat of the van, and the two men scrambled inside. As the stranger walked away, the big man began to whimper in fear.

"Virgil, wh . . . what'd he mean, 'last moments'? What'd he mean? I'm . . . scared . . ."

"Shut up you fool. You think you're the only one scared? What was I supposed to do, jump him?"

"You may continue with your repairs," he said to Kevin, who tried to move but couldn't. "Do not fear. All is well now," he urged gently. "Your wife and friend are unharmed."

Cathy sprang forward and embraced Kevin, who reached out and found Carl's hand behind her. "This is not happening!" he said, half to himself.

"As soon as I stop shaking . . . I'll help you ch-change the tire," Cathy said.

The giant walked to the front of the van and looked into the front seat, still holding the shotgun in his left hand. Neither he nor the occupants moved for the ten minutes it took Kevin to change the tire. A dozen more vehicles passed on the highway without slowing down. When he heard the trunk lid slam, he returned to the car.

"Go in peace now. You shall have no more troubles on your journey."

"Sir, I . . . I don't know how to thank you . . ." Kevin began. "We'll call the police at the next exit . . ."

"There will be no need for that." He looked at

Carl when he spoke the words, and only Carl noticed the slight nod of his head.

"Children, we must go now," Carl urged. Kevin helped him into the car, and then slid behind the steering wheel, drawing Cathy close to his side. She leaned her head against his shoulder and spoke in a whisper.

"Just drive away, Kevin, and let's find a place to lie down."

The car rocked gently onto the travel lane and quickly accelerated. Only Carl looked back through the rear window. The tall figure was turning toward the van.

"God Almighty! God Almighty! What's he going to do?" the big man cried.

"Shut your mouth, you fool!" the little man snapped between short breaths.

He was before them now and he seemed to grow larger and larger. His clothing became flowing robes of white and his hair and skin began to glow until all around him there was blinding light.

"Lucifer!" he called with a voice of thunder. "Come! Claim your minions! Their evil shall cause no more sorrow on this land!"

His eyes looked upon the van and the two men cowering inside. "Be gone!" he thundered. "To the bottomless pit—be gone! There you shall dwell forever in the misery of your master!"

From out of the valley came a ball of fire, and a hideous laugh rumbled through the ground as the fire surrounded and consumed the van.

The driver of the tractor-trailer rig slowed his vehicle as the tiny flicker of light touched the shoulder of the road just beyond the beam of his headlights. He strained his eyes as he sought the source. Then, shaking his head, he chided himself at the sight of the large crow perched atop the guardrail. He didn't notice the rising wisp of smokey haze.

10

LILLIE WOKE with a start and twisted her neck uncomfortably to find the lighted face of the alarm clock that had become a part of her torment. The hands read two-twenty. She had slept for over three hours under the sedation of the drugs Dr. Needy sent with the health nurse—drugs, she had been assured, that would take her through the long night ahead. But the one with the yellow eyes mocked the power of man's pitiful medicines; in the stillness, he had come to her again. She could see him now as she looked past her feet. He glided to the bedside and her head turned to meet him. But this time, as never before, she knew that she was not rendered mute.

"Yeeees, wretch," he chortled, "I have given you your tongue in my presence this night, and I trust that you are duly honored."

Lillie's lips parted a fraction of an inch and she drew in a labored breath. "Please . . . ju-just leave me be."

"Oh, but I cannot. I have developed an intense attraction for you, wretch that you are, and I must be fulfilled. Perhaps I rushed you during our first work together; sometimes, in my excitement, even I miscalculate. But there is always another time, another opportunity."

"Not here, there's not," she whispered loudly.

"Yes, I am aware that you removed the filthy little beggars, but *you* are here. You have spoiled pleasures untold for me through the years." His voice now gushed the hatred as he no longer attempted to mask it. "Though there are others that merit my personal attention, I shall stay with you until the rot of your flesh is a fragrance unto my nostrils in this very room. *You* . . . and your *teeen*der heart and your *loooving* ways, groveling with the little maggots as if you could undo my handiwork!"

The words stung her like a lash and she could feel the tears begin to spill from her eyes. "I . . . I never . . . believed you existed . . ."

"How stupidly mistaken you were. How did you think your maggots came to such sweet sorrows? By the imaginations of the dull creatures from whence they sprang? Hardly! Few grant me the credit I deserve on this earth, but I can wait; one day there will be much time to honor me."

Lillie could see his thin smile in the weak light, and a spark of courage welled in her. "Say what you want . . . but I did some good for them. I . . ."

"Oh, you give yourself far too lofty a position in the scheme of things. 'Good' you say! What is

STEVEN W. WISE [189]

'good'? Nothing but a stupid human word! Do you not comprehend how easily I can erase your 'good,' how easily I can return them to the hands of others who would do my bidding? And, then, oh pleasing thought, do you not know how I am able to make *them* befoul their own offspring one day. You did *nothing* for them, save postpone the inevitable."

He bent his head close to hers, and for the second time, she knew the reek of him. Her terror pinned her motionless to the bed.

"But even for this postponement, I shall extract my price, wretch, and it shall be great. You will come to hate your maggots, for without them, it is unlikely that you would have ever displeased me to the point of personal attention.

"Your torment shall extend one hour beyond the dawn, and the next day, two hours, and the next, three . . . I trust you are able to understand the progression? And when your screams of agony begin to spew forth, I will render you mute so that the fools who attend you will not know of your torture."

He withdrew from the bedside with a scratchy laugh, and his voice grew quiet again, as it was when he first came. "It is only four hours 'til the dawn. This will be your last brief night. And since I desire that you should remember your little maggots for a while longer, I shall postpone your pain for yet another hour this night. Use it well, wretch. If you manage to hate them a bit, I might foreshorten your agony even longer."

Her thoughts turned to the children, but not as he had wished. She caressed the memory of each, and the hour passed swiftly before the rending of her flesh forced her into a sweaty knot.

♦

Kevin drove the remaining distance to Asheville, North Carolina, in one hour and a half, and took the first exit off Interstate 40, pulling into the parking lot of a small motel. Not a word had been spoken since the incident in Tennessee. Child-like, Cathy had remained snuggled against Kevin's shoulder. She had scarcely moved, even though he knew she had not slept.

He returned from the front desk with two room keys and handed one to Carl as he climbed back into the car. He heard Carl squirming in the back, digging for his wallet.

"We'll square up later, Carl. Don't worry about it now," he said tiredly. "Got two side-by-side down at the end of the building."

Kevin soon had Carl situated in his room, and as he turned to leave, the old man's voice stopped him.

"Son . . . I'm so sorry I got you all mixed up in this . . ."

"Hey, it's all right, Carl. None of it was your fault. . . . We'll talk in the morning."

After a fitful four hours of sleep, Carl woke as the first sliver of light cut through the crack in the curtain. He made his way to the bathroom and spread

STEVEN W. WISE   [191]

one of the bath towels on the floor in front of the vanity. Half leaning against the wall, he bathed himself as best he could and then rubbed his dripping body with another of the thin white towels. He dressed quickly and pulled open the curtain before sitting in the padded chair beside the small table. His thoughts crowded against one another in a rush, and he passed his hands slowly over the sides of his bowed head. Several things were clear to him now. The one he sought was not an ordinary woman. The forces of evil had been unleashed in an attempt to stop him. Only by what he was certain was an angelic visitation, had they been thwarted. The lives of two innocents were now a part of it all, and the thought that he had not properly judged the gravity of the situation gnawed at him. True, their rescuer had promised them safety for the remainder of the journey, but Carl knew that he had no right to expect Kevin or Cathy to understand all that was taking place. And he certainly was not at liberty to allow, much less encourage, them to continue. He would complete the journey alone, at least as far as human beings were concerned. He sat for an hour before he heard stirrings in the next room, and it was another half hour before he answered the knock on his door.

"Morning, children," he said as they came into the room. "You both look a little better this morning."

"Yeah, I guess we do, even if we didn't sleep much," Kevin said.

"Hear me out for a minute, and then I want you to drive me to a bus stop. I'll be forever sorry I got you mixed up in this. I . . . I should have known better. But that's done and I can't change it now. At least you're all right. You've both been far more than friends for the last few weeks, and I'll always remember you—always. But now, I'm going on alone to finish this thing, and I've got to go now. Please go home, or on to the coast if you still feel like it. Just take me to a bus stop. We'll ask the desk clerk where to go."

He rocked forward in the chair, but before he could get up, Cathy spoke. "There's no need for apologies. We're adults, and we made this decision ourselves—practically made you let us drive you. So just drop that, okay? We talked it out this morning . . . and we're taking you all the way down there."

Carl opened his mouth to protest, but her hands and eyes begged for silence.

"What happened back there on the highway . . . Some of it we understand . . . and some we don't. The world's full of bad people. . . . We've just never run into any that bad, but, hey, why not us? It could have been anybody."

She paused and looked at Kevin, taking his hand in hers. "But . . . *him*. That we don't understand, and in a way, that scares us more than the men with the gun. No normal man could've done what he did to the door of that van. And he just came up out of nowhere in the middle of the night. . . . I mean . . . and the men, what happened to them? We're

STEVEN W. WISE   [193]

not the most religious people in the world, but . . . Well, we just want you to help us understand."

She shook her head, annoyed she couldn't better articulate her thoughts.

"I'll tell you what I think, children. Lord knows, you deserve at least that. No, he wasn't a normal man. He wasn't even a man at all. Most people, when they think of angels, think of little kids, all dressed up in white gowns with little wings, like children in a Christmas pageant. But that's not so. I believe we were saved by an angel of God, sent to us in the form of a man. That's what I believe."

"And if that's so, Carl, you and the woman you're trying to find must be awfully important?" Cathy asked.

"She is. I know that now. . . . *She* is. There're powers that fight over good and evil all around us in this world, most of it unseen. But, just because we don't see it, doesn't mean it isn't real."

"Carl, we just know part of it—about the cloth and the old Bible," Kevin said, "but we want to know the whole story. We know it's a personal thing, and maybe we shouldn't ask. But, after what we've been through with you . . . well, we just hope you'll tell us everything, because, like Cathy said, we're going on down there with you. There's no use trying to talk us out of it. We want you to find her, too, and four more good legs and a car will do a whole lot better than that one leg of yours."

Carl smiled at both of them in turn, and considered the crossroad that was upon them. He could stand his ground, unshakably this time, and force them to leave him. But he knew he would not, in fact, could not. He had not forgotten the promise of the angel. No more harm would come to them on this journey. He was sure of that. He told them of his mother and the articles of faith; he told them all that he knew himself; and he told it with all the passion that was in him.

When he finished, they were bound in spirit and in love—bound to one woman long dead and to another who lived whom they had never seen.

♦

The breeze, drifting in from the northeast and the cool waters of the Atlantic, thirty miles east, caressed the throbbing temples of the woman seated at the second-story window. Every few moments, the delicate zephyr shifted its course and the woman's face moved to receive it lovingly, thankful to the power that induced the wind to touch the ocean. The old chair protested with faint creaks as its rockers glided back and forth over the carpet. The sound mingled with the swish of broad oak leaves and came to the woman's ears as song. She accepted the offerings from the window and willed her thoughts away from the hour to come and toward the one whose room she now occupied. Scores of children lived briefly in this room and had taken solace from it. But it was now and forever Kay's

STEVEN W. WISE   [195]

room, no matter how many more would pass through it after Lillie Crow was dead.

Susan and the nurse had been gone for an hour. They had helped her bathe and had attempted to feed her, but neither act of kindness was meaningful. Somewhere in the darkness of the previous night, he had taken another part of her, and only the strongest of odors could be detected in her nostrils. And then only faintly. The nurse had given her an injection with instructions to remain in bed until sleep came, but she had left the bed with the sound of the car engine. It had required nearly all of her strength to walk to Kay's room and drag the rocking chair to the window, but it did not matter now. She would not return to the other bedroom. She had slept her last night on the rack of torment and she had seen the yellow eyes come from the wall for the last time. If the fiend were to find her this night, he would find her in death.

She lowered her eyes to the glint of sunlight touching the blade of the knife resting on the windowsill. Susan had brought a food tray up from the kitchen with a dull dinner knife. For a moment, Lillie had considered slipping it from the tray, but then the night in the twin's bedroom came back to her. She remembered the kitchen knife and the thud of the handle against her foot as it dropped from her hand. She knew it must have bounced forward, under the bed. And it was there, two feet under the bed, unnoticed until her fingers found it again.

It would be a simple thing to do—not even a

mess for Susan to clean up, no carpet to replace. One more short walk to the bathroom, draw a tub of comforting hot water, and then, with all the strength that remained, thrust the blade up and deep just under the juncture of her rib cage. There would be one last moment of pain before she fled from him forever.

And so, Lillie sat in the friendly sunshine and drank in the breeze and the music of the oak tree. There was no hurry; nightfall was three hours away and he never came early. She tilted the small perfume bottle, soaking the corner of the white handkerchief clutched in her other hand. And, as the breeze shifted directly into her face, she lifted the cloth to her nostrils and inhaled deeply. The scent comforted her.

◆

Kevin lifted his foot slightly from the accelerator and glanced at the speedometer needle as it dropped to forty-five miles per hour. The city limit sign for Washington, North Carolina, stood like a lonely sentinel on the shoulder of the highway and quickly passed from view.

"This is it, Carl," Kevin said over his shoulder. "Want to grab a sandwich somewhere?"

The sense of urgency had been growing with alarming speed during the last hour, and with it a claustrophobia born of the tedious miles. More than anything, Carl wanted to be alone, to breathe fresh air and feel the warmth of the late afternoon sun-shine on his face. He desired a place to seek her in prayer.

"I'm not hungry, son. What I'd like for you to do is to stop and ask where the cemetery is, and then take me there and leave me for a while. You two can go get something to eat and come back and pick me up. Okay?"

He watched as Kevin and Cathy exchanged brief looks in the front seat. "It's okay, children, I'm thinking straight," Carl said. "It's my favorite place to think and pray, and I'm afraid we don't have long."

Kevin pulled into the parking lot of a conve-nience store and left the engine idling as he slid from the seat. Two customers were waiting to pay for purchases, and he fidgeted as the clerk labori-ously filled out a gasoline ticket. The woman in front of Kevin clutched three bags of potato chips in the fingers of her left hand and a quart of milk in her right as she shouted to her son, lingering at the shelves of candy.

"Pick something out *now*, young man, or you'll lose your chance. Hear me?"

The child whined with exasperation as the rows of brightly colored wrappers begged for his fingers, and his dirty tennis shoes danced in place.

"Uh, excuse me, ma'am." Kevin's voice dis-tracted her from the boy. She half-turned to meet the stranger. "I'm from out of town, and . . . I'm looking for the cemetery. I wonder if you . . ."

"Which one?" the woman huffed.

"Well, I didn't know there were two of them in . . ."

"Ain't two of them. They's three. Two pretty big ones and a little Catholic one." Her head darted toward the boy. "Jeremy Coates, if your chubby little paw ain't wrapped around a candy in the next ten seconds!" She turned back to Kevin as if no interruption had taken place. "Well?"

"Uh . . . Actually I don't care which one. The closest one will do," Kevin said.

The woman's eyes narrowed as she contemplated this strange request, and Kevin felt a mounting discomfort.

"If you've come to flower a grave, how can you not know which graveyard it's in?"

"Well, that's not exactly why I . . . Uh, we're looking for . . . one, ma'am," Kevin stammered.

Her eyes grew stern and the disheveled head of black hair shook slowly. "Why else would a stranger look for a graveyard?"

"It's an old fellow that's with us, really. He needs to get away and think for a while, he says. Does it best in a cemetery."

"That so?"

"Yes, ma'am, that's the truth."

Her glance traversed Kevin from head to foot within two seconds. "You look too old to be up to any mischief, I reckon . . ."

"Honest, ma'am, there's no mischief about any of this, I swear. Could you just tell me . . ."

"Ain't far, Shepherd's Cemetery. Go about a mile that a way." She gestured with the milk carton. "Couple more stop lights and turn right on Turner Road. Half mile or so on your left. Can't miss it."

"Thank you kindly, ma'am," Kevin said as he moved to the door. The woman did not reply.

Kevin plopped onto the car seat and yanked the gear selector down a notch into reverse, and maneuvered the car down the driveway, quickly finding a break in the highway traffic.

"It's not far," he said. "Turns out there's three of them. This one is the closest."

He followed the woman's directions and five minutes later the wrought iron gate of the entrance loomed in the distance. The car turned onto the gravel driveway and stopped fifty yards into the gray sea of monuments.

"This is fine, Kevin," Carl said. "Give me half an hour or so. Go get something to eat. I'll be right around here somewhere. I won't go too far."

Carl watched as the tires raised two small columns of white dust and the car turned onto the asphalt road beyond the gate. He dug his crutches in the gravel and began to make his way between the headstones.

The car quickly slowed and stopped at the curb, a quarter mile from the entrance gate.

"You hungry?" Kevin asked.

"Not a bit," Cathy answered knowingly.

"Let's go back and take the second driveway where we can see him. He'll never know."

Cathy reached for his hand and gave it a quick squeeze as the car pulled back onto the road.

The slanting rays of light filtered through the green mass of tree limbs bordering the west edge of the cemetery. The old man leaned silently on his crutches as he faced the shafts of light. He had hobbled away from the road, through row after row, and the passing vehicles were reduced to soft whooshes which did not distract him. After long moments, he moved near the trunk of a massive green ash tree and carefully lowered his weight to its base, rocking his shoulder blades against the rough bark until he was one with the tree. He raised his face to the sunlight again as he began to pray.

◆

The woman peeling potatoes at the sink raised her head to the familiar rumble of the pickup as it came up the driveway. She rinsed her hands and dried them on the dishtowel hanging on the oven door handle. It was much too early for him to be coming in; something must have broken. As she reached for the kitchen door, she hoped it was not something expensive. She could see that his hands were free of grease as he strode toward the house, his head down in thought, and she knew his preoccupation was not with things mechanical.

"What's wrong, Ernest?"

STEVEN W. WISE   [201]

"You remember that boarder Mable brought to services last Sunday?" he asked quietly. She nodded. "Something passed between us . . . I'm not sure what, Wilma, but he came to me again just now, out there in the pasture. I feel the need to pray for him, for what he's trying to do . . . whatever it is. It's no small thing, of that I'm sure."

She could see the weight of the burden in his clouded features, but he would not have to bear it alone. Without a word she clamped an arm around the dirty coveralls and walked into the house with him. Saturday night supper would be an hour late on the small farm six miles north of Paducah, Kentucky.

◆

He did not know how long he had been sitting at the base of the old ash tree, but it did not seem like a long time. His body protested as he struggled to gain leverage and rise on his good leg. He used a crutch handle for a hand grip as it leaned against the tree trunk. He tottered for a moment before trusting his balance and securing both crutches in his armpits. The sunbeams slanted ever lower and the fiery edge of the great ball had dropped below the far tree line in submission to the approaching night. Carl figured he had spent at least an hour at the tree; sixty precious minutes had been pared from the woman's life. He had prayed mightily with every fiber of his being, but he had been given no clue to her whereabouts. Yet there was no panic about him, only resolve.

"Seek, old man," he whispered to himself, "and ye shall find. . . . Ye shall find."

The worn tips of the crutches dug into the lush turf as he retraced his steps to the driveway. The car was waiting for him, Cathy and Kevin standing outside and leaning against the door.

"Have you been waiting long?" he asked.

"No, not so long," Kevin answered. "We've been thinking. It seems like a hospital or maybe a nursing home would be a good place to start hunting. What do you think?"

Carl considered the suggestion for a moment as he allowed his gaze to sweep over the long lines of soft marble hues. Somehow it didn't feel right. A sense of loneliness crept into his thoughts. Irritated at the selfish distraction, he attempted to force it from his mind, but it wouldn't budge. Then he realized that it was not his isolation that troubled him, but hers. The woman was alone.

"It's a good thought, children, but it doesn't feel right. She's not with other people. She's by herself somewhere, I'm sure."

"What do we do, then?" Kevin asked. "Seems like we ought to have a plan or something. This looks like a fair-sized town." He shook his head slowly as he looked into Carl's face.

"Let's just ride for a while, okay?" Cathy offered. "We haven't seen anything yet but a cemetery, and we know she's not here. Maybe Carl will feel something if we pass near where she lives. Let's find some residential areas before dark. I'll write down the street names so we won't cover the same ground twice. Won't be any place to find a map on Saturday night; we'll just have to do the best we can."

"Let's ride," Carl said.

The car moved slowly down one residential street after another as Carl's head swiveled from the houses on the left to the houses on the right. But they were nothing more than rectangular chunks of brick and wood, devoid of any particular sense of foreboding. They rode for an hour. The only conversation in the car came in brief phrases or syllables as the cool air took on a dampness and crept through the half-opened windows.

Carl sighed wearily, and both Cathy and Kevin heard the distress in it. "Whew . . . I feel bad about losing this first day," he said.

"It was only a few hours of the first day," Cathy reassured him. "We'll get our heads together tonight and come up with something in the morning. Don't worry."

"Ah . . . I don't know," he replied. "I hate to give up this first day." He huffed with irritation. "Kevin, you just as well pull back on a main road for a bit. I've got to use the bathroom."

The dark orange letters of a Hardee's sign jutted over the curbing of the four-lane street as Kevin wheeled into the drive and took a parking space near the entrance.

"We'll wait here," Kevin said as he opened the

door to help Carl from the back seat. The old man hobbled into the restaurant.

"Cathy, I swear, this doesn't seem to make any sense."

She shook her head and raised her hands from her lap before releasing them with a plop. "Don't bug him tonight, Kevin. He's tied up in a knot. We'll all think better in the morning."

Carl leaned his weight against the heavy swinging door of the air lock and shouldered his way onto the sidewalk. Then a shrill cry froze him to the concrete, and the cloth at the base of his neck prickled the leathery flesh. The grating call came again from the opposite side of the building. "Caw . . . caw . . . caw."

Carl quickly made his way around the front of the structure and as he rounded the sharp corner of bricks, he spied the black feathers, lustrous, even in the fading light of evening. The bird ceased its calling and stood statue-like as its beady eyes sought the man. It was perched atop a frame bulletin board positioned in the strip of lawn just beyond the outside edge of the parking lot, near a small cluster of picnic tables. Some of the flyers and notes flapped in the breeze like an infant's clothing hung on a clothesline to dry. He began to move toward the bulletin board, coming within six feet before the great bird extended its wings and thrust its way into the sky. Carl crutched closer to the board and began to study the handbills. Automobiles and boats for sale, kittens for free, church benefits, estate auc-

STEVEN W. WISE [205]

tions, roommates sought, upcoming musical events and shows—all begged for his eye and attention. Carl studied them all, devouring every word and address, every photocopy and caption, but none held any meaning for him. He re-checked the board carefully, left to right, top to bottom, until he was satisfied he had seen them all. He felt the breeze freshen and shift slightly from behind him and a flapping at the lower right corner of the board caught his eye. The red of the small leaflet had faded to a watery pink behind a larger paper that had been tacked over it. He reached for the top handbill and folded it up, pinning it against the board as his eyes searched the older one hidden beneath. The lettering was blocky and, though badly weathered, still legible.

ITEMS NEEDED FOR BAKE SALE TO
BENEFIT
CROW HOUSE. APRIL 10, ON FRONT LAWN.
1634 MORNINGSIDE ROAD.
CALL LILLIE CROW
FOR ARRANGEMENTS. 452-7892.

Carl's heart pummeled his rib cage and his eyes blurred with moisture as he reached out and tore the paper from the thumbtacks. He pivoted wildly on his right crutch, barely maintaining his balance as he lurched toward the car.

Both Cathy and Kevin sprang from the car at the

sight of his haste, fearing he would surely fall before he reached them.

"We've *found her*, children. Praise God, we've *found her!*"

"Slow down, Carl, easy." Kevin reached to steady him.

"We've got to get to a phone. I think I saw one in there. Give me a quarter, somebody." The sentences punched the air breathlessly.

Three figures hovered over the pay telephone as the coin dinged its way downward.

"Put in the number, Cathy. My hand's shaking too bad," Carl said, and she punched the seven digits.

"It's ringing," Carl whispered. "Please answer, Lillie Crow . . . Please answer . . ."

◆

The alien noise came from behind the woman, and it rang three times before she identified it. Susan, she thought as her brain responded to the intrusion. Susan or the nurse. It had to be one or the other. No, not the nurse; she would think her asleep from the shot. It was Susan. One last check for the evening. The phone was on the nightstand. She would wonder why Lillie didn't reach over and answer the call. Lillie doubted she could reach the phone within a full minute; possibly in two or three —too long, she knew. Susan would come; but it

STEVEN W. WISE   [207]

didn't matter. It was almost time anyway. The shadows had crept over the yard far enough.

The woman at the window forced herself to inhale deep breaths of the cool air as she gathered her strength. She leaned forward and placed the perfume bottle on the windowsill and picked up the knife, bringing it to her lap and stealing a glance at the keen steel edge of the blade. For a moment, she began to doubt her resolve. She could see herself wrapping her arms around Susan and being taken from Crow House. Maybe he would not pursue her in another place, and maybe . . . But her eyes returned to the shadows of the yard. Shadows fell everywhere, and wherever she fled, there would be shadows before nightfall. He would come from one of them, and he had promises to keep.

She had at least fifteen minutes. That would surely be time enough, she assured herself. The ringing from her bedroom stopped, and the silence was welcome.

11

CARL BANGED the telephone receiver back into its cradle and passed a hand over his forehead and through the shocks of gray hair.

"How do you know it's her?" Cathy asked.

He turned to look through the window at the bulletin board and did not reply for several moments. "A black angel showed me," he said softly. He began to say more and then waved his hand as if to dismiss further mention of the subject. Instead, he said, "Kevin, go to the counter and ask directions to this Crow House place. Cathy, let me in the trunk of the car while he asks. Okay?"

Cathy took the car keys from Kevin and opened the entrance door for Carl as Kevin went to the service counter. The trunk lid was up by the time Carl caught up with her. The paper sack was tucked deep into the corner of the cramped space. Cathy lifted the corner of a suitcase and pulled the small brown package from its resting place.

"Thanks," Carl said, turning to wait for Kevin who was jogging across the parking lot.

"It's at the northeast end of town, off the main highway," Kevin called. "Street called Morningside Road, about a mile past the Gull Lane intersection. She said it'd take about ten minutes to get there."

"Let's ride," Carl urged.

♦

Lillie reached for the windowsill with her left hand as she rocked forward from the chair and stood on wobbly legs. The view from the window whirled, and an instant before falling, she managed a step to the wall. She let her back bump heavily against it. A full two minutes passed before she attempted to open her eyes and take a tentative step, still keeping her free hand on the wall for support. Slowly, she slid her hand down the wall until it was free and took a second step; then two more. She reached the doorway to the bedroom and leaned against the frame until the dizziness subsided again. She repeated the painful process—moving from the bedroom to the middle of the hallway—and then completed the last leg of her journey from the hallway to the bathroom. She knelt beside the tub and laid the knife on the shining porcelain edge, placing it carefully, so that it would not be knocked off when she entered the water.

She reached for the faucet and turned on the water full force. It splattered coldly on her face and she recoiled from the shock. But warmth came quickly and soon a comforting stream tumbled from the faucet as she adjusted the balance. The cascading water was like a tiny waterfall and she focused on the close sound, attempting to cleanse her mind of all else. Her eyes were fixed on the water level as it inched upward, and she chose a black speck on the wall of the tub as the final marker. The tiny waves rocked, clear and clean, until they bathed the spot.

She pushed up from the edge of the tub and tested the water. It bit her fingers and she jerked them free and reached for the cold water knob. The plunge of water again filled the small room, and covered the sound of a car pulling into the driveway. She couldn't hear the heavy slamming of automobile doors.

The water was fine now, and she stepped into the warmth. The hem of her blue gown swirled colorfully, clinging to her ankles. She eased her body into the water, allowing the penetrating heat to caress her skin. Soon it lapped over the nape of her neck and stroked the lowest curls of hair. The fingers of her left hand sought the handle of the knife, and after she had secured it, she transferred it to her dominate hand.

"Look around back, Kevin," Carl instructed as he negotiated the front porch steps.

"There's a car back there, but there's nobody outside," Kevin called as he emerged from the corner of the house.

In the space of twenty seconds, as many images

STEVEN W. WISE   [211]

flashed through Lillie's mind in silent, movie-like fashion—children's faces, sullen and tearful; Susan's face, her dark eyes flashing at the misery of a child; white bandages wrapped about tiny limbs; bruises like ugly stains in grotesque shades of black and yellow. They all exacted their toll. Maybe the evil one was right after all. The adrenaline pounded through her body, and her heart pulsated like a living creature struggling to free itself from the prison of her chest. It was time now.

With trembling hands, she directed the point of the blade until it pierced the thinness of the wet gown and she could feel the faraway prick of metal on her flesh. The doorbell chimed from below. Then there was loud knocking on the door, growing louder, but her grip did not slacken.

"Susan . . . oh, Susan," she whispered. "I'm sorry I wasn't braver for you . . ."

The agonized cry of a man's voice commanding, "Kick it in, Kevin! Now!" came to her with the crashing of the front door. The sounds reverberated through the house.

Then she heard him again. "Lillie Croooow! Lillie Croooow!"

It was the anguish in his cry that stayed the blade —anguish born of one who was about to lose his own life. Yet it was hers he cried for.

"Please! Let me talk to you. Pleeease!"

She looked down at the knife, the blade nearly buried under the bloody water, the steel of a half inch was lost in her flesh. The sight of her own gore gave new strength to her will for death, but the voice would not leave her to her purpose.

"In Jeeesus name! Pleeease hear me out!"

She heard the scuffle of footsteps, running all about the floor below her, and images of the past tangled with the voice. The footsteps were pounding now, ascending the steps. The face of a young man appeared in the doorway, his mouth half-opened with horror at the grisly sight. The blur of another figure, someone much smaller, brushed past him and turned to stone a yard from the tub.

"Don't . . . don't do it . . . please." The earnestness in the young woman's voice made Lillie pause. She neither thrust the knife deeper nor withdrew it.

Carl had discarded his crutches at the foot of the staircase and half-drug his body to the top, as he fought the incline while still clutching the sack in his left hand. The plaster foot of the cast clumped heavily on the floor outside the bathroom, and then he burst into the tiny room as Kevin jumped outside the doorway, making room for him. Carl's jaws clenched involuntarily at the unreal scene, but he ignored the trembling hands on the knife and the crimson water. He sought only her eyes. Still an arm's-length from the edge of the tub, he spoke softly, barely above a whisper, as his fingers popped the tape from the sack.

"Miss Crow . . . it'll be all right now. . . . Yes, ma'am . . . all right now. . . . In Jesus' name, it will . . . I promise . . ."

STEVEN W. WISE   [213]

The Bible and the frame of cloth were free and Carl carefully placed the worn text on the edge of the tub with his left hand. He eased his bulk to the floor, the cast stretching awkwardly to the wall. Then, with both hands in his lap he twisted the frame until a sharp crack filled the silence. His fingertips found the cardboard backing, tearing it away from the cloth, and as he worked, his eyes did not leave Lillie's. She had made no sound since they had come.

He touched the cloth and his fingers gathered the small patch to his palm. Cautiously, he joined his hands, raising them to the top of the tub, and inched his way forward on his knees.

"Lillie Crow, I've come a long way to find you. I've brought you a gift from my mother. . . . She was sick once too . . . a long time ago, but she was made well. And you can be, too . . . if you'll just give me a chance."

She found her voice, but it was little more than a rasping sound, nearly unintelligible. "Who . . . are you?"

"A friend in Jesus, Lillie."

Strong hands closed over hers and she offered no resistance as they took the knife. Her arms shook from the strain of the past several minutes, and Carl guided them to her body. He stared at the point from which the blood leaked into the water and lowered her hands over it.

"Hold to your body, sister. . . . Hold tight."

Carl withdrew his hands from hers and knotted

them against his chest. "Oh, sweet Jesus," he prayed, "hear my cry of faith. Let the blade do no harm to this woman, driven to the brink of death by Satan's dark powers. Give us time together here in this place . . . time to tell her of You."

The soft rumble of his words was soothing. Lillie noticed that her hands no longer trembled. The cruel sting in the center of her body began to lose its energy, and then it was gone.

Carl turned to Cathy, her face pale and drawn with tension. His lips silently signaled for her to come to the tub and she moved forward.

"Miss Crow, my young friend here is a nurse, and I want you to let her tend your wound. Would that be all right?"

Lillie's head turned and her eyes focused on Cathy for a moment before she nodded her approval. Carl moved aside and allowed Cathy to take his place.

"Just . . . just let me take a quick look, Miss Crow," Cathy said as her fingers found two buttons of the gown. Gently, her fingertips parted the garment and she strained to find the wound.

"I'm going to drain a little water from the tub. Okay? I can't see very well."

Mutely Lillie nodded and Cathy waited as the water level crept downward revealing white flesh at the top of the gown opening. Halfway down the opening, still Cathy could see only fair skin. Finally the bottom of the opening was exposed, and still there was no wound. She allowed the water to con-

STEVEN W. WISE   [215]

tinue draining and unbuttoned another button, carefully probing with her fingers. She reached to the stopper and jerked it upward. The three buttons were re-fastened by shaking hands.

"There . . . is . . . no cut on her. No mark of any kind." And as she spoke, Cathy stole a glance at the bloody water.

"Praise You, sweet Jesus," Carl said. "To Thee be the glory . . . Yes, Mighty Lord . . . yes. Cathy, find us some dry towels. Miss Crow, we're going to get you dried off now and out of this bathroom, all right? Kevin, son, come in here and take my place. Help Cathy get her up and out of the tub."

Kevin picked his way into the room and first helped Carl to his feet and out into the hallway. As soon as Lillie was out of the tub and seated on the toilet lid, Kevin left her alone with Cathy and joined Carl outside the door. "Get my crutches, will you, son?"

Within a few moments, Cathy called through the closed door.

"It's okay now, Kevin. Come back and help me."

Strong arms steadied Lillie as she emerged from the room she had never intended to leave.

"Where's your bedroom, Miss Crow?" Cathy asked.

Lillie motioned to her right. "Down there. But I want to go to that one." She moved her head the opposite direction, toward Kay's room. The cluster of bodies inched forward until Lillie was secure on the edge of Kay's bed.

"Sit with her, Kevin, while I find a dry gown from her bedroom," Cathy instructed. She quickly returned. "You two step out for a minute and we'll get changed."

When the door opened again, Lillie lay in the middle of the bed, her head and shoulders propped up on two pillows. Cathy had pulled a chair close to the side of the bed and she motioned for Carl to take it. He made his way to the chair and sat down.

"Kevin, would you go get my Bible, please. I believe we're going to need it after a while."

Kevin disappeared into the hall and returned with the Bible, extending it to Carl's outstretched hand.

"Thanks, Kevin."

Cathy stepped to Kevin's side, taking his hand, and the couple began to walk to the door.

"No, please, children, stay with us," Carl said. "See if you can find a couple more chairs. We're all together now . . . all the way through this."

They quickly returned and took places slightly behind Carl. He reached behind him and touched their joined hands.

Lillie studied the three strangers before her and the dream-like aura about her began to recede. Her eyes sought Carl's, and she found his gaze steadfast and full of tenderness. The young couple looked upon her with equal kindness, but their eyes lowered from time to time in deference. She smiled inwardly at their innocence, and the seed of compassion stirred within her. Her fingers clutched the damp cloth and, fully aware of it now, she looked at

STEVEN W. WISE   [217]

it for the first time. Her fingers opened like flower petals to the sun and she gently stretched the cloth to its full extent. Her blood had given it a pinkish cast and it looked to her as if it had always been that color. Her thoughts continued to take form, clearer now, and questions formed in her mind, but for a moment she was unable to speak. The man saw her attempt, she was sure of it, and the flicker of a smile lit his face before he spoke.

"Reckon we ought to introduce ourselves, Miss Crow." The smile was full now. "My name's Carl . . . Carl Whittenburg. I come from Missouri. These young folks here are Cathy and Kevin Hatfield, and they are from Kentucky. Strange as it all must seem, ma'am, we've come with one purpose, and that's to help you in Christ's name."

He paused, waiting for a moment to give her a chance to speak if she wanted to. He decided she didn't, but before he could speak again, she raised the fingers of one hand. He waited.

"How . . . how do you know who I am?"

"It's sort of a long story, and some day I'll tell it all if you want to hear it. But, for now, just know that I was led by powers greater than mine."

"How did you know that I was . . . about to . . . ?" Lillie stammered.

"A feeling of dread came over me. It was so strong that it almost felt like I was dying. It was just made known to me."

She turned her head from him and a wave of

sadness passed over her features. Her gaze was fixed at some random spot on the ceiling.

"You saved me . . . but not for long."

"Miss Crow, I know you have a terrible sickness. I knew that from the beginning. That's what we've come for—to help you deal with it."

"There'll be no dealing with it. . . . It's a cancer, spread all over my body. It would have been better if you'd let me die in there."

"No, ma'am . . . no. You've got to stop thinking that. How is it that there's no mark on you where the knife cut you?"

Lillie's hand reached for her stomach, and she remembered the pain and the blood. "That was just a scratch that stopped bleeding on its own," she said evenly.

"Miss Crow, have you ever read any Bible stories?"

Lillie shook her head. "Not since I was a kid."

"Would you listen to one now, if I read it to you?"

"If you've gone to this much trouble to find me, I reckon you can do whatever you want."

Carl's fingers found the marker and he opened the book and began to read. He read the story as if for the first time, pouring every fiber of his being into Saint Mark's narrative about the dying woman and her faith. When he had finished, he laid the open Bible on the bed near Lillie. She revealed no emotion; her stare had returned to the spot on the ceiling.

STEVEN W. WISE   [219]

"This woman was as bad off as you are, Miss Crow. All else had failed her; she had nothing left but faith. But that was all she needed."

"Seems to me she had Him . . . close enough to touch," said Lillie. Her statement came as a surprise to Carl, who had wondered if she'd even listened to him read.

"Yes, ma'am, He was there . . . close enough to touch as you say, and His body is not here now. That's true enough. But when Christ left this earth, He didn't leave us alone and He didn't take His power with Him to paradise. He left the Holy Spirit here with us and the same power that healed the woman two thousand years ago is here, too."

"It's a beautiful story, Mister Whitten . . ."

"Let me tell you about another sick woman, one that didn't live two thousand years ago," Carl said earnestly, "not even a hundred years ago. I don't claim to know the whole story, but I do know that she was near death, likely as close as you think you are. She thought of this healing that took place, and she cried out to God for the same power as the woman's touch of Christ's robe. . . . And she received it . . . because she believed. She got up from her death bed and lived for sixty more years."

Lillie was looking at Carl now, searching the deep-set eyes watching her from under the bushy brows.

"This woman was my mother, Miss Crow. I know these things to be true. And I know that the cloth you hold in your hand was in the room with her that day. Oh, it's been trimmed to fit in the frame, but it is of the same garment that she held in faith. As far as I know, only she and one other woman ever knew exactly where it came from, and they both died without telling. But I saw what those two women did through their faith. Mind you, they never healed anybody in their lives—ever. Nobody else who has ever lived has either. They had the gift of telling others how to touch Christ, so *He* could heal them. Don't you see? Touching that cloth will help you know Him. It's like a link in a chain, sort of. Touch it and know my mother's faith, and start to build some of your own. . . . There's more than enough for you, too. . . . In the precious name of Jesus . . . know that."

Carl's head slowly bowed to his chest and the rough flesh of his hands came together with the sound of sandpaper as the fingers interlaced. The only sound in the room was the whisper of his prayer.

The gleam of the street light high above Morningside Road did not reach into the gloom at the edge of the back yard, nor did it reach the two figures, standing ten feet apart. The shorter of the two spoke first and his voice trembled with hatred.

"How is it that one of your exalted position should stoop to watch over a simple wretch such as she?"

"Thou knowest the reason, Satan." The taller one's reply was gentle.

STEVEN W. WISE   [221]

"He does not have her yet," Satan hissed, "for I have worked mightily with her, and she knows of my power."

"She will soon know of our Lord's power."

"*Our* Lord? *Your* Lord. Do not include me! I honor no lordship save my own, you know that."

"A great pity, that. It did not have to be so."

"Bah! I have no time for idle talk with you. Leave her to me; she is of no great import to His Majesty." The words dripped with sarcasm. "I am working with others in high places, as you must know. I will barter you one of your choosing for her; no two, and you must surely recognize the bargain."

There was no hesitation in the angel's reply. "I shall remain."

"I will do all within my power to give you regret at your decision."

"This I know, Satan, and I also know this. Thy time is fleeting, and my heart is gladdened with the thought. Be gone with thee!"

The yellow eyes narrowed to slits and vile curses spewed from his mouth. The last curse ended in a high-pitched wailing that slashed through the night air like the cry of a wounded animal.

To Cathy and Kevin, the sound was that of a coyote, strangely close to the house. But not to the man praying and the one for whom he prayed. Lillie's skin began to crawl with the knowledge that her tormentor had returned, but as the howl faded away, the dread within her ebbed also. With the silence came an assurance, as keen and pure as love itself, that he would not return to her. Carl extended his hand to hers and squeezed it for a moment. She could see his head nod as he tapped into her peace.

"We're alone now," he whispered.

"Yes . . . yes . . . I know," she replied. She shifted the cloth into her left hand, reaching for the Bible with her right, and her fingers brushed the thin pages. "Read it again, would you, please? I think I want to hear it once more."

Carl's voice filled the room with a new vibrancy, and he struggled not to shout with joy as he cherished each word he quoted, his eyes fixed on Lillie, not once looking at the page.

"I've always believed in something good, something loving," Lillie said when he finished. "God, I reckon . . . or my version of Him, maybe. . . . I don't really know. But I've seen a lot of what hate can do."

She paused, searching for the right words. "I . . . I've come to know the one . . . who's behind it all—the evil—and that's why I was going to kill myself. I . . . I was running from his torment. I had given up."

"He's been defeated!" Carl said. "He can hurt you no more. You know that now, don't you?"

"That's what it feels like, yes, and I hope it's true."

"It is true, Miss Crow. Love is stronger than Sa-

STEVEN W. WISE   [223]

tan, stronger than hate, stronger than death, stronger than . . . cancer."

Carl looked behind him at Cathy and Kevin and motioned for them to draw near. "These are fine young people, Miss Crow. Some day soon you'll want to get to know them better, I promise. They're going to be parents for the first time soon, and a lucky child it is, I can tell you that. I want them to gather round you with me and join hands . . . all of us. You hold on to that old cloth while we pray, and just believe. Don't wonder if you can be better, just have faith that Jesus is as mighty today as He was for the woman in the Bible, and as He was for Momma."

Kevin went to the other side of the bed and sat on the edge while Cathy took a place on the bedside near Carl. Carl raised his hands and extended one to Lillie and one to Cathy. Then he began to pray.

"Oh, mighty Lord, hear our prayer for this woman who needs you so. Our hands are as clay; there is no power in them to heal . . . that power is Thine alone . . . and only fools pretend otherwise. We seek no power or glory for ourselves, and know it would be wrong to do so. We ask only that You hear our humble cries, and take pity on us in this fleeting life. Reveal Yourself to this good woman. We know she stands for great goodness because we have seen the power of Thine hand as we were lead to her, and we know that Your plan for her is not finished. Oh, come, Lord Jesus . . . now as we wait on Thee. . . ."

Carl's voice trailed to a whisper, and there were other whispers in the room. One came from the trembling lips of Lillie Crow. "If I may but touch His clothes, I shall be whole."

The circle of hands remained unbroken for several minutes until Lillie released her grip. She looked in turn at the three faces, and smiled at each. "I feel a weariness now that's very heavy, and I think I need to sleep. Bring your things in and make yourselves at home. There are plenty of bedrooms to use, and food is in the kitchen if you're hungry. I . . . I need to be alone. I hope you understand."

Cathy helped Carl to his feet and Kevin met them. Together they quietly made their way to the door and closed it behind them after turning off the overhead light. Lillie pulled the top pillow from behind her and sank into the bed. The Bible remained on the bed and the light from the street lamp filtered into the room, bathing the open pages with a soft luminescence. She raised the cloth to her lips and kissed it, and spoke the words again as sleep took her. "If I may but touch His clothes, I shall be whole."

With the clean wind of midnight, the angel knew his vigil was over and he moved from the edge of darkness toward the house. The only light came from the living room. He could see the old man's profile, slumped in a chair. He was not asleep; every few moments his lips moved and the bushy hair protruding above the chair would bob in unison with the knot of hands in his lap. The angel moved closer, and when he stood beside the porch railing, he stopped and smiled gently. "Thou mayest take thy rest now, beloved."

Carl's head found the soft corner of the chair and his hands relaxed as sleep took him. All-seeing eyes swept about the big house for the last time and then a powerful rush of air cleansed the yard and sang through the trees as the angel departed.

Lillie opened her eyes as the muted light of dawn began to overcome the darkness of the bedroom. She drew long, eager breaths of the fresh air that whispered through the window, each breath deeper than the one before. There was no pain. She lay comfortably on her right side for the first time since it all began. She stretched her body to its full length and she turned to her back. Cautiously, almost timidly, she probed the side of her right breast, but the only sensation was the firm pressure of her fingertips.

Lillie Crow covered her face with her hands and wept quietly. Soon the tears of joy found the creases along both sides of her face and followed them to the pillow. She found the Bible with her fingers and closed it over the square of cloth. "Sweet Lord Jesus, what's left of my days . . . I offer back to You and the kids. My life is Yours and theirs."

She arose from the bed and stood to perfect balance before walking to the bathroom and turning on the water at the lavatory. She cupped her hands and splashed the coldness to her face, relishing the shock of it. When she reached for the towel the bright object caught her eye. The knife lay on the floor beside the tub, strangely out of place. She knelt and picked it up. She laid the thick bath towel on the floor and folded it carefully over the knife until she was satisfied it was secure, and then she placed the bundle in the bottom of the metal waste can under the lavatory. She took another towel from the closet and set about drawing a tub of water for her bath. When she had finished bathing, she combed and brushed her hair and tiptoed to her bedroom. A soft splash of green in the closet caught her eye and she dressed quickly. The sight of her image in the light green print dress nearly caused her to laugh at the mirror. It had been many days since she had cared about such matters, and she smoothed the dress lovingly.

After she had returned to Kay's room and retrieved the Bible with the cloth inside, she walked to the top of the stairs and looked down into the living room at the sleeping man. For the first time, she noticed the plaster-covered leg, jutting whitely to the floor, and then the crutches leaning against the chair. She descended the stairs noiselessly and walked to the couch near his chair and sat down. Part of him was aware of another presence in the room and soon he stirred in his uncomfortable resting place.

STEVEN W. WISE   [227]

"Good morning, Mr. Whit . . . Whittenburg, isn't it?" Lillie said.

He rubbed the slumber from his eyes and straightened his posture as he focused on the woman before him. She wasn't the same woman he'd seen the night before. Her eyes were beacons, deep and penetrating, and the features of a strong, yet feminine, face materialized in the soft light. With both hands she held the Bible and cloth in her lap. His eyes asked the question silently, but he knew the answer even before he saw the delicate nod of her head.

"Praise be . . . Miss Crow. Praise be," came the choked voice, and he extended his hand to her. She left her chair and walked to him, offering her hand. He kissed it tenderly.

"Mr. Whittenburg . . ."

"Carl, please, ma'am."

"Carl it is. Lillie, for me, all right?" He nodded.

"Carl . . . there are a hundred questions that I want to ask you, and I don't even know where to start."

"Miss, ah, Lillie, there's not that much to tell, and I'm not just saying that. I was directed by the hand of God Himself . . . not because I'm who I am, but because of who you are. Tell me about what you do here."

"This is a home for abused and abandoned children. I . . . I've been looking after them for many years, until . . . I got sick."

Carl smiled and nodded. "I knew you had a lot to do with love. . . . I knew that for sure."

"Never had children of my own, but . . . I have loved many children . . . many."

She looked down at the Bible in her lap and ran her fingertips around the worn edges before offering it to Carl.

"No, ma'am . . . they're yours now. They're where they belong."

"Carl, I can't keep these things. They must mean the world to you, please . . ."

"They belong to no one, Lillie . . . not me, not even my mother when she had them. Someday, and I don't know when or how, you'll pass them on to someone in need. You'll know when the time comes . . . just like I did."

She opened the Bible and touched the cloth with one fingertip. "I wonder . . . where it came from."

"There was a time when I was younger, that I burned to know the answer to that, but no more. All Momma would ever say was that it was ancient. 'Ancient is the cloth' she would say with a twinkle in her eye. And that's enough for me. It'll have to be enough for you, too."

"It's enough, Carl."

"I imagine this house will be full of children fairly soon, huh?"

"I suspect it will." She smiled broadly.

"We'll be leaving as soon as I can get the young folks up and about."

"Oh, no, not that soon, surely. Let me fix . . ."

STEVEN W. WISE   [229]

"It's better this way, Lillie. I know that people will be coming to check on you soon . . . and, well, I don't want to get caught up in all the clamor. And there'll be clamor sure as soon as your friends lay eyes on you."

"But without you all . . ."

"Without us, it would have been somebody else. Lord wants something done, He gets it done. Us or some other folks, it doesn't matter. I'd rather leave quietly, if you don't mind."

"Well, at least leave me an address and a phone number. I can't imagine not talking with you again."

Lillie jumped to her feet and disappeared into the kitchen, returning with a small pad of paper and a pen.

"I'll write while you stir the kids, all right?" Carl said.

She nodded and walked to the stairs while Carl began to write. When she returned he handed her the tightly folded note and she slipped it into the pocket of her dress. They talked for several more minutes while busy footsteps hurried across the up-stairs floor. Cathy came down first, followed closely by Kevin, who held a small suitcase. As Lillie stood to greet them, Cathy's mouth half-opened at the sight of the tall woman whose face no longer wore the pall of doom. The voice that had awakened them sounded strong, and Cathy knew that some healing had taken place. But this sight was more than she had dreamed possible.

"Different, huh, kids?" Lillie smiled at them, extending her hands.

Cathy took her hands and shook her head as tears welled up and spilled onto her cheeks. "I . . . I don't know what to say. I . . ."

"I'm the one who should say something, sweetheart," Lillie said and drew her in and hugged her. "You, too, young fellow. Thanks seems like mighty little, but it comes from the bottom of my heart, believe me. Promise me you'll at least send pictures of your baby and write? Okay? I want to know all about you. You found your way down here once; surely you can do it again sometime."

Carl had his crutches in place. "We'd best be moving on now, children," he said.

Lillie followed them to the door and out onto the porch. "It doesn't seem right . . . after all that's happened, for you to go this way," she said.

"In a few days, when this place is full of kids like it ought to be, it'll seem right then, Lillie. Trust me."

She swallowed hard at the thickness in her throat, and could not utter a reply as they neared the car.

"One favor I might ask, Lillie," Carl's voice boomed across the yard.

"Anything," came the faint reply.

"I suppose you had a doctor?"

"Yes . . . sort of."

"When he asks you about what happened . . . just tell him to read the fifth chapter of Mark. Will you do that?"

"I'll do it, Carl. I promise."

She watched until the car had disappeared down the street before she pushed open the mangled door, walked into the house, and picked up the telephone in the kitchen.

"Hello," she heard Susan say, and Lillie was barely able to restrain herself from shouting her joy, but she steadied herself before answering.

"It's Lillie."

"Are you all right? What's wrong? Lillie?" the questions shot rapid-fire from the receiver.

"Calm down, honey, I'm all right. Yes, I'm all right. Listen, I want you to come over a little later on. No hurry."

"Lillie, you . . . sound different. Do you feel better?"

"Yes, Susan, I feel much better. You can see for yourself when you come. Plan to stay for a good while. Okay?"

"I'll work it out, Lillie. Give me an hour."

"Great. Susan, would you do me one other favor?"

"Name it."

"See if you can go by and pick up Kay and bring her with you. I want you two to find out together."

"Find out *what?* Lillie Crow, what's going on over there?"

"It's good, Susan, it's real good. See you in an hour."

Lillie smiled as she hung up the phone and imagined the whirlwind she had just created across town.

Her fingers found the note in her pocket and she sat at the kitchen table as she unfolded it, the blocky penmanship mannish as it glared from the paper.

I do not know the address I will soon have, but it will not be far from yours. I will save the first thousand years so we can talk. Keep loving many children. Until that day.

Carl

She re-folded the note and pushed her chair from the table. Her head was held high and her back was ramrod straight as she climbed the staircase and walked to her bedroom. If anyone had seen her, they would have thought her stately in her short walk. She opened the top dresser drawer and withdrew a small jewelry box, gently lifting the lid. She looked at the two wedding bands that lay side by side, golden against the purple backdrop. She took the larger of the two from the box and after clutching it in her hand for a moment and whispering her husband's name, curled the note inside the ring and returned it to the box.

Her eyes found the calendar above the nightstand and she stared at the rows of blank squares representing the last month. She tore the page from the calendar and watched triumphantly as the strong fingers of her right hand reduced it to a tiny ball. Then she tossed it into the wastebasket.

STEVEN W. WISE

Epilogue

THE LIGHT that flooded paradise was brilliantly white, but it did not offend the eyes of the two angels. The lesser of the two hovered near his mentor and took note of the aura of exceptional joy about him, his great head slightly tilted and bowed toward earth.

"Thy rapture this day is joyful to behold, Archangel. I would humbly seek to know of it."

The head slowly turned, the celestial visage capturing the radiance full force.

"I return from earth with glad tidings. Saint Cora's cloth has been given to another, and this hour I have told her of the event. It was my privilege to watch over her son, who diligently sought the afflicted woman."

The great angel's voice was tranquil, yet resonant, drifting about the place, and soon the airy whir of wings grew near as other angels gathered.

"The healed woman, Archangel, did she know the Christ before the man found her?"

"She knew Him not," was the somber reply, but the voice quickly regained its vibrancy. "It is an earthly life extended for the good of many children, and more: a soul was taken from the enemy."

A harmonic murmur arose from the circle of angels now close by, and it increased to a crescendo that wafted through the heavens until the archangel motioned for silence.

The subordinate angel raised his face to the exalted one and spoke again. "I beg thee, Archangel. Tell those who do not know of the cloth of Saint Cora."

In the silence, a thousand radiant faces sought the archangel, and he lifted his head majestically as he began to speak.

"In the year of her salvation, Saint Cora fell to a plague inflicted by the Prince of Darkness. It was a grievous illness, and the blood flowed from her body until she lay in the shadow of death. She cried out to our Lord in great faith and sought to touch His garment and be healed, just as another woman did long ago. The Spirit caused her eyes to fall upon the hem of her own garment, and in that instant, she knew His might. She clutched the garment, and wept joyously, and by faith was healed. She removed a small portion for safekeeping, and many were healed as they were led by the cloth to faith in our Lord Jesus. And so it shall be when it is passed to another by Saint Lillie."

"Archangel." The words were nearly whispered.

STEVEN W. WISE   [235]

"It would be my great honor to attend Saint Lillie in the hour of her coming."

"Thou hast pleased me this day. When her labors are complete, the honor shall be thine."

The murmur from the throng again swelled in loud chorus, and the melodious sound was pleasing to the heart of God.

About the Author

Steven Wise, a graduate of the University of Missouri, is a licensed real estate appraiser. He is a deacon in his church and teaches a junior high class in Sunday school. He lives in Columbia, Missouri, with his wife, Cathy, and their two children, Travis and Stacee.

Midnight is his first novel.